THE OVERNIGHT KIDNAPPER

After a hectic morning, Inspector Montalbano arrives in his office ready to find out what's troubling Vigàta this week. What he discovers is unnerving. A woman on her way home from work has been held up at gunpoint, chloroformed and kidnapped, then released hours later — unharmed and with all her possessions — into the countryside. Later that day, restaurant owner Enzo tells Montalbano that his niece has recently been the victim of the same crime. Before long, a third instance has been reported. As far as Montalbano can tell, there is no link between the attacker and the victims. So what is this mystery assailant gaining from these fleeting kidnappings? Montalbano must use all his logic and intuition if he is to answer these pressing questions before the kidnapper finds his next victim . . .

THE OVERNIGHT KIDNAPPER

ANDREA CAMILLERI

TRANSLATED BY STEPHEN SARTARELLI

LARGE
PRINT

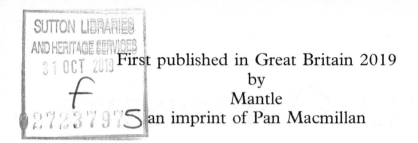
First published in Great Britain 2019
by
Mantle
an imprint of Pan Macmillan

First Isis Edition
published 2019
by arrangement with
Pan Macmillan

ISBN 978–1–78541–786–3 (hb)
ISBN 978–1–78541–792–4 (pb)

Published by
F. A. Thorpe (Publishing)
Anstey, Leicestershire

Set by Words & Graphics Ltd.
Anstey, Leicestershire
Printed and bound in Great Britain by
T. J. International Ltd., Padstow, Cornwall

This book is printed on acid-free paper

CHAPTER
ONE

At half-past five that morning — give or take a few minutes — a fly that had long been stuck to the window-pane as though dead suddenly opened its wings, rubbed them together to clean them, then took flight and, a moment later, changed direction and landed on the bedside table.

There it kept still for a few seconds, taking stock of the situation, then shot away like a rocket, straight into the left nostril of the placidly sleeping Inspector Montalbano.

Without waking up, the inspector felt a bothersome itch in his nose and slapped himself hard in the face to make it go away. Since, in his groggy state of sleep, he hadn't gauged the force of the blow, it had two immediate results: one, it woke him up; and two, it smashed his nose so hard that it started to bleed.

He bolted out of bed, cursing the saints in rapid fire as the blood gushed out, dashed into the kitchen, opened the fridge, grabbed two ice cubes, applied them to the bridge of his nose, and sat down, keeping his head bent back.

Five minutes later, the bleeding stopped.

He went into the bathroom, splashed some water on his face, neck, and chest, and then got back into bed.

He had barely closed his eyes when he felt the very same itch as before, except that this time it was in his right nostril.

Apparently the fly had decided to change its area of exploration.

How was he ever going to get rid of this tremendous pain in the arse?

Using his hand really wasn't the best idea, given the earlier result.

He shook his head gently. Not only did the fly not move, it went further inside.

Maybe if he scared it . . . "Ahhhhh!"

The yell left his ears ringing, but it achieved the desired result. The itch was gone.

He was finally starting to fall back to sleep when he felt the fly again, this time walking on his forehead. Cursing the saints again, he decided to try a new strategy.

Grabbing the sheet with both hands, he tugged it sharply, pulling it completely over his head. That way the fly wouldn't find so much as a millimetre of exposed flesh to walk on. The problem was that by shutting himself in like that, he cut off most of his air supply.

It was a very short-lived victory.

Less than a minute later, he distinctly felt the fly land on his lower lip.

It was clear the disgusting insect hadn't flown away but had remained under the sheet. He felt suddenly disheartened. He would never win his battle with the damn fly. "A strong man knows when to admit defeat," he said to himself, getting out of bed in resignation and going into the bathroom.

After returning to his bedroom to get dressed, just as he was about to take his trousers from the chair where he'd left them, out of the corner of his eye he saw the fly on the bedside table.

It was within reach, and he took advantage.

In a flash he raised his right hand and brought it down on the fly, crushing it so thoroughly that it remained stuck to his palm.

He went back into the bathroom and took a long time washing his hands, humming all the while and feeling satisfied with his revenge.

But when he strode triumphantly back into the bedroom, he froze.

A fly was walking over his pillow.

So there must have been two flies! But then, which one had he killed?

The innocent one or the guilty one? And if he'd killed the innocent one by accident, would this mistake come back to haunt him one day?

Would you please drop this nonsense? he said to himself. And he started to get dressed.

Drinking a large mug of coffee, he put on his last articles of clothing, looking sharp as a clasp knife, opened the French windows, and went out onto the veranda.

The day looked just like a picture postcard: a beach of golden sand, a turquoise sea, and a deep blue sky without so much as a hint of cloud. He could even see a sail far out on the water.

Taking a deep breath, Montalbano filled his lungs with the briny air and felt reborn.

To his right, at the water's edge, he noticed two men standing and quarrelling. Although he was too far away to hear what they were saying, he could tell, from the agitated way they moved their hands and arms, that they were having a heated argument.

Then, all at once, one of them made a move that Montalbano didn't get a good glimpse of at first. He seemed to bring his right hand suddenly forward, causing it to flash in the sun.

It was clearly a clasp knife in the man's hand, but the other blocked it with both arms crossed and in the same motion kneed his adversary in the balls. The two men then grabbed each other bodily, lost their balance, and fell, all the while struggling fiercely and rolling around in the sand in each other's clutches.

Without thinking twice, the inspector hopped down from the veranda and started running towards them. As he drew near he began to hear their voices.

"I'll kill you, you bastard!"

"And I'll cut your heart out and eat it!"

The inspector was out of breath when he caught up to them.

By this point one man already had the upper hand and was straddling his opponent, pinning the other's open arms with his knees, practically sitting on his stomach and battering his face with punches.

Just to be on the safe side, Montalbano dealt the top man a powerful kick in the side, unsaddling him. Caught by surprise, the man fell onto the sand, yelling:

"Look out, he's got a clasp knife!"

The inspector turned around quickly.

The man who'd been on the ground was now getting to his feet, and indeed he had a clasp knife in his right hand.

Montalbano had made a big mistake. The more dangerous of the two men was the one who'd been on the ground. But he didn't give him time even to open his mouth. With a kick to the face he sent him down to the ground again on his back, in the same position as before, as the clasp knife flew a good distance away.

The other man, who had stood up again in the meantime, immediately took advantage of the situation to jump on top of his opponent and resume punching him.

Everything was back to square one.

So Montalbano bent down, seized the puncher by the shoulders, and tried to pull him off the other. But since the man put up no resistance, the inspector himself lost his balance and fell back, belly up, as the puncher crashed down on top of him.

Then, fast as lightning, the man with the clasp knife jumped on both of them at once. The puncher was kicking wildly, trying to hit the inspector in the balls, as Montalbano pummelled him with his left fist while with his right he hammered the man on top of them both, who was trying in turn to blind the inspector with one hand and do the same to his adversary with the other.

They looked, in short, like a giant ball with six arms and six legs flying out as it rolled along the sand, a ball yelling curses, smacking punches, shouting threats, and dealing kicks. Until . . .

A voice, very close and imperious, commanded:

"Stop or I'll shoot!"

The three men froze and looked.

The person who'd shouted was a lance corporal of the carabinieri, pointing a sub-machine gun at them. Behind the corporal was another uniformed carabiniere, holding the clasp knife. Apparently they'd been passing along the coastal road parallel to the beach, seen three men brawling, and intervened.

"Get on your feet!"

The three men stood up.

"Move!" the corporal continued, gesturing with his head that they should walk towards a large jeep parked along the road with a carabiniere at the wheel.

To tell or not to tell? Montalbano asked himself Hamletically as he walked along towards the van, wondering whether he should reveal the fact that he was a police inspector.

He came to the conclusion that it was best to tell the truth and clear up the mistake at once.

"Just a minute. I am . . ." he said, coming to a stop. The whole group also halted and looked at him.

But the inspector was unable to continue, because at that very moment he remembered leaving his wallet with his police ID in the drawer of his bedside table.

"So, you gonna tell us who you are?" the corporal asked sarcastically.

"I'll wait and tell your lieutenant," Montalbano replied, and he resumed walking.

Luckily the rear of the jeep was covered by a tarpaulin; otherwise, the whole town would have seen Inspector Montalbano ride past in the custody of the carabinieri, and the laughter would have been so loud they would have heard it all the way to the Italian mainland.

Once inside the carabinieri station they were escorted in less than gentle fashion into a large room, where the corporal sat behind one of the two desks.

He took his time, adjusted his jacket, stared long and hard at a ballpoint pen, opened a drawer, looked inside, closed it, cleared his throat, and finally began.

"Let's start with you," he said, addressing Montalbano. "Show me some kind of ID."

The inspector became anxious, realizing the situation was getting rather sticky. Better change the subject.

"I had nothing to do with the dispute between these two men," he declared in a steady voice. "I intervened to break it up. And these two, whom I don't even know, can confirm that."

He turned and looked at the others, who were standing three paces behind him, guarded by a carabiniere.

Then something strange happened.

"All I know is that you kicked me in the side and it still hurts like hell," said the puncher.

"And you kicked me in the face," said the man with the clasp knife, pouring it on.

7

Suddenly Montalbano understood everything. Those two bastards knew perfectly well who he was and were now trying to make trouble for him.

"I'll make you stop wanting to play the wise guy in a hurry," the corporal said menacingly. "Give me that ID."

There were no two ways about it. Montalbano had to tell the truth.

"I haven't got it with me."

"Why not?"

"I left it at home."

The corporal rose to his feet.

"You see, I live in a small house right . . ." The corporal came and stood directly in front of him. ". . . right by the sea. And this morning I . . ."

The corporal grabbed him by the lapels of his jacket.

"I'm a police inspector!" Montalbano shouted.

"And I'm a cardinal!" the corporal retorted, as he started shaking the inspector back and forth, making his head bob like a ripe pear about to fall.

"What's going on here?" asked the carabinieri lieutenant and station commander upon entering the room.

Before answering, the corporal gave Montalbano one last violent shake.

"I caught these three brawling on the beach. One of 'em had a clasp knife. And this one here claims he's —"

"Did he give you his name and address?"

"No."

"Let go of him at once and show him into my office." The corporal looked at his superior in confusion. "But . . ."

8

"Corporal, I gave you an order!" the lieutenant said sharply, cutting him off and leaving the room.

Montalbano mentally congratulated him. The lieutenant was saving them all from ridicule. He and the inspector knew each other very well.

As they were walking down the corridor, the bewildered corporal turned to Montalbano and asked him in a soft voice:

"Seriously, though, are you really a police inspector?"

"Not on your life!" Montalbano reassured him.

After everything had been cleared up and the lieutenant had given his apologies, which took about ten minutes, Montalbano left the carabinieri compound.

He had no choice but to go home and change his clothes. In the scuffle he'd not only got sand in his private parts, but had also torn his shirt and lost two buttons from his jacket.

The best thing to do was to go to the station, which was barely a fifteen-minute walk away, and get somebody to give him a lift home.

He headed off.

But he felt pain in his left eye and right ear, and he stopped in front of a shop window to look at himself. He'd taken a hard punch square in the eye, and the skin around it was now starting to turn blue. On his ear he could clearly see the imprints of two teeth.

As soon as Catarella saw him, he let out a yell that didn't seem human so much as the cry of an injured animal. Then he let loose with an avalanche of questions.

"Wha' happened, Chief? 'Salt wit' a deathly weppin'? Or a 'salt wit' a reggler weppin'? Was ya hambushed?

Eh? Wha' happened? A car crash? A splosion? A fire wit' criminal intint?"

"Calm down, Cat," the inspector interrupted him. "I just fell. Any news here?"

"Nah, Chief. Oh, but a jinnelman come by 'is mornin' wantin' a talk t'yiz poissonally in poisson."

"Did he tell you his name?"

"Yessir, 'e did. Alfredo Pitruzzo."

He didn't know anyone by the name of Pitruzzo. "Is Gallo in?"

"Yessir."

"Tell him I want him to give me a lift home. I'll wait for him in the car park."

Pulling up at the house, he noticed a car parked next to his. He said goodbye to Gallo, opened the front door, and went inside. Hearing him, Adelina came out of the kitchen, looked at him, and started yelling, just like Catarella.

"*Matre santa*, wha' happen a you? Eh? Wha' happen? My Gah, what a mornin'! What a terrible mornin'!"

What was Adelina talking about? Why was she saying these things? What was so terrible about the morning? What could have happened?

"What do you mean, Adeli?"

"Isspector, when I come inna this mornin', the whole a house a was empty, abannoned, you wasn't here anna French window was open. A criminal coulda come in anna steal everytin'. An' when I was inna kitchen, I heard someone come in fro' the veranda. I tought it was you an' so I come out anna look. But it wasn't you, it

10

was a man an' 'e was lookin' aroun'. I was sure 'e was a burglar an' so I grab a fryin' pan an' I come a back out. An' since 'e had 'is back to me I whack 'im inna head wit' a big fryin' pan, an' I knock 'im out! An' so I tied 'is hands an' feet wit' a rope, an' I gag 'im an' I put 'im inna broom cupboard."

"But are you sure he was a burglar?"

"'Ow should I know? Bu' sommabuddy 'oo comes inna sommabuddy ellis's 'ouse . . ."

"But why didn't you call me at the police station after you knocked him out?"

"'Cause first I 'adda take a care o' the *pasta 'ncasciata*."

Montalbano appreciated her answer and went and opened the door of the broom cupboard. The man was crouching and looked at him with terrified eyes.

At first Montalbano was convinced the man couldn't be a burglar. He looked about sixty years old and was well dressed and well groomed. The inspector helped him to his feet, and after he removed the gag, the man immediately shouted:

"Help!"

"I'm Inspector Montalbano, police!"

The man seemed not to hear.

"Help!" he shouted, even louder than the first time. And now he started shaking all over.

"He . . . he . . . help! He . . . he . . . help!"

The man no longer knew what he was saying, and there was no way to get him to pipe down. Montalbano made a snap decision and put the gag back on him.

Adelina, meanwhile, had come running from the kitchen and was standing beside the inspector.

The man's eyes were so wide with fear that they looked as if they might pop right out of their sockets at any moment. Since he was clearly too terrified to think straight, it would have been a mistake to untie him.

"Give me a hand," the inspector said to Adelina. "I'll get him by the shoulders, and you get his feet."

"Where are we taking him?"

"We're going to put him in the armchair in front of the television."

As they were carrying him like a sack of potatoes, the inspector worked out a version of events in the hope of making the best of a bad situation. After they'd sat the man down, Montalbano asked him:

"If I have her bring you a glass of water, do you promise not to scream for help?"

The man nodded. As Montalbano was removing the gag, Adelina returned with a glass of water and had him drink it, a few small sips at a time. The inspector did not put the gag back on him.

After a few minutes had passed, the man seemed to have calmed down and was no longer shaking. Montalbano pulled up a chair and sat down in front of him.

"If you don't feel up to talking, just answer me with gestures. Do you recognize me? I'm Inspector Montalbano of the Vigàta Police."

The man nodded.

"So how can you think that I, who don't even know you, would want to do you any harm? What reason would I have to do that?"

The man just looked at him as though unsure.

12

CHAPTER
TWO

So the inspector started speaking in the most persuasive tone of voice he could muster.

"I think it must all have been an unfortunate coincidence. This morning, due to a series of unexpected circumstances, I had to go to the carabinieri station and didn't have time to close and lock my French windows. Apparently someone saw that there was no one at home and came into the house to steal something. As luck would have it, though, a few minutes later, you came in, too. At which point the burglar — we'll call him that even though he didn't have the time to steal anything — struck you, tied you up and gagged you, and put you in the cupboard. But then Adelina, my housekeeper, came in, and so the burglar was forced to run away empty-handed. I'm sure that's exactly how it all went. Do you believe me?"

"Yes, I believe you," the poor man said in a faint voice.

Montalbano then bent down to untie the rope around his ankles, after which he freed his hands.

With some effort, the man stood up. But he still hadn't fully recovered his sense of balance.

"If I may," he said. "My name is . . ."

Then suddenly he fell back onto the armchair, shaking all over and as pale as a corpse.

"Are you unwell?"

"I feel dizzy and have a really bad pain here, where I was hit."

And he brought his hand to a spot at the nape of his neck. Adelina ran into the kitchen and returned with some ice cubes wrapped in a piece of cloth, which she had him put on the aching spot. The man moaned softly in pain.

Montalbano got very worried. Adelina was a strong, robust woman, and it was possible that her blow with the frying pan had caused the man some internal injury.

"Please remain seated and don't move," he said to the man. And he ran off and phoned the police station.

"Cat, is Gallo there?"

"Yeah, 'e's onna premisses, Chief."

"Tell him to come back to my place."

He hung up and turned his attention back to the man. "I'll have you taken to the hospital."

"I wanted to tell you . . ."

"Please don't talk . . . don't make any effort at all."

"But it's important for me to . . ."

"Whatever you wanted to tell me you can tell me this afternoon at the station, all right?"

Five minutes later the doorbell rang.

Spurred by the inspector's urgency, Gallo, who always loved to drive as though every country road was the track at Indianapolis, had practically flown there.

As Montalbano stood blissfully under the warm, long-awaited water of the shower, he started thinking about that morning of mix-ups.

14

He'd mistaken the more dangerous man, the one with a knife, for the weaker one; the carabinieri had mistaken him for a brawler; and Adelina had mistaken an honest man for a thief. And since trouble always comes in fours — he thought, coining a new phrase — he became absolutely certain that very, very early that morning, he had killed an innocent fly, mistaking it for the guilty one.

Before leaving the house, he looked at himself in the mirror, as was his habit. He had a dark circle around one eye, just like a clown at the circus, and a swollen ear.

No matter. He wasn't exactly entering a beauty contest.

"Did Gallo ever come back?" he asked Catarella upon entering the station.

"Yessir, Chief, 'e got back jess now. How d'ya feel?"

"Great."

"Can ya tell me sum'n, Chief?"

"Sure."

"Seein' as how ya got a black eye 'n' all, wha'ss the woild look like tru' that eye? Is it all black?"

"How d'ya guess, Cat? Now, tell Gallo to come to my office."

Gallo appeared at once.

"How'd things go at the hospital?"

"Fine, Chief. All they found was a large contusion, so they gave him some painkillers and I drove him home. He told me to tell you he'll be coming here around four this afternoon."

Gallo had just left when Mimì Augello came in.

He took one look at the inspector, smiled, then assumed a serious expression, made the sign of the cross, brought his hands together in prayer, bent at the knee, pretending to genuflect, and raised his eyes to the heavens.

"What's this little comedy routine for?"

"I was saying a prayer of thanksgiving for whoever it was that gave you a black eye."

"Stop being an idiot and sit down."

At that moment Fazio came in without knocking. He was frowning and looked upset.

"Chief, sorry to ask, but was it the carabinieri who put you in that state?"

Montalbano felt mortified.

How on earth had the story already spread all over town? The gossip and laughter couldn't be very far behind. And if the news ever reached the commissioner's ears . . .

"I don't believe it! You were arrested and beaten up by the carabinieri?" Augello asked angrily, springing to his feet.

"Just calm down, everyone," said the inspector. "Don't go jumping to conclusions, because there really is no reason to be declaring war on the carabinieri. I can explain everything."

And he told them the whole story, down to the fine details. When he'd finished, he asked Fazio: "And how did you find out?"

"Marshal Verruso, who's an acquaintance, told me in strictest confidence."

Montalbano heaved a big sigh of relief. That meant the story would remain confidential.

16

"Any new developments?"

"At my end of things, there was just a stolen car whose owner didn't realize it was gone until he got back from abroad," said Augello.

"I, on the other hand, have an interesting story to tell," said Fazio.

"Let's hear it."

"Late last night, after the rest of you had gone home, a man showed up here, a certain Agostino Smerca, to report something that had happened to his daughter Manuela."

"And what was that?" Augello asked impatiently.

"This Manuela, who's a rather attractive woman of thirty — Smerca showed me a photo of her — lives with her father, who's a widower, in a small house a bit off the beaten track. She's a cashier at the Banco Siculo and gets off work at six-thirty every evening. Since she doesn't like to drive, she takes the circle line and then has to walk for another ten minutes to get home. About a week ago — actually, five days ago, to be exact — after getting off the bus, she was walking along the road, which is almost always deserted, when she saw a car stopped with its bonnet raised and a man looking at the engine. Just after she walked past it, she felt the barrel of a gun pointed into her back, scaring her nearly out of her wits, and heard a man say: 'Don't scream or I'll kill you.' Then she felt him press something over her nose and mouth, which turned out to be a handkerchief or gauze pad soaked in chloroform, after which the poor woman passed out."

"So why did this Smerca wait all this time to report the incident?" asked Augello.

"Because his daughter didn't want him to. She didn't like the idea of everyone in town talking about her."

"Was she raped?"

"No."

"Robbed?"

"No."

"So what'd the guy kidnap her for?"

"Well, that's just it. In fact he didn't do anything at all to her. Nothing. The woman woke up again an hour and a half later, out in the open countryside. Her handbag was right beside her, and when she opened it, nothing was missing. So she tried to get her bearings, realized where she was, and called a cab from her mobile. And there you have it."

"Maybe he'd mixed her up with someone else," said Augello.

Hearing mention of another mix-up, Montalbano, who'd been silent up to that point, gave a start. Not another mix-up! One more on the same day, and he just might lose his mind. He wanted to say something, but then thought better of it and remained silent.

"I guess it could have been any number of other things," Augello continued. "What's this Smerca do for a living?"

"He's a businessman. A textile wholesaler."

"There you go. Maybe he missed a payment to the protection racket. They were sending him a warning."

"Mimì," said Montalbano, finally entering the discussion, "if this was a Mafia case, you can be sure

18

Smerca wouldn't have come and reported it to us. He would have worked it out on his own."

"That's also true," Augello agreed. "And what if the girl just made the whole thing up?"

"Why would she do that?"

"Maybe as an excuse, to explain to her father why she was getting home late . . ."

"Come on! A woman of thirty, in this day and age?"

"And what do you think?"

"At the moment I don't think anything. But I do smell something fishy. The whole thing doesn't make any sense. I'd like to talk to this girl in person — but just her, without her father around."

"If you want, I'll ring her and tell her to come here this afternoon. What time would be best for you?" asked Fazio.

"I've got an appointment at four. But it shouldn't take long. Five would be fine."

Entering the trattoria, he immediately noticed that Enzo, the owner, didn't seem his usual jolly self. He looked rather taciturn. Since Montalbano considered him a friend, he asked him: "Is anything wrong?"

"Yes."

"Feel like talking about it?"

"If you would be good enough to give me fifteen minutes of your time after you've eaten, I'll tell you everything."

"Just tell me now."

"No, sir."

"Why not?"

"Because eating, like sex, wants no worries."

In the face of such ancient wisdom, Montalbano could only submit.

In fact, he had himself a feast, just to spite the carabiniere corporal who had arrested him.

When he had finished, Enzo took him into a windowless cupboard next to the kitchen and closed the door. They sat down in two half-collapsed wicker chairs.

"What I'm about to tell you took place six nights ago, but my brother Giovanni just told me about it yesterday afternoon. Giovanni has a thirty-year-old daughter, Michela. She's a level-headed girl and works at the Banca di Credito."

Montalbano had a sudden intuition.

"Was she by any chance kidnapped and released shortly afterwards perfectly safe and sound?"

Enzo looked at him in amazement. "She certainly was. But how did you —"

"Another very similar incident occurred the very next day. I would like to talk to this niece of yours."

"My niece is right here. I called her after you said you could give me a bit of your time."

"Go and get her."

Enzo went out and returned with a good-looking brunette with a serious air about her. He introduced them to each other.

"If you don't mind," the inspector said to Enzo, "I would like to speak to her alone."

"I don't mind," said Enzo, going out and closing the door behind him.

The young woman clearly felt awkward and intimidated.

20

The inspector beamed her a big smile of encouragement. The girl replied with a forced smile.

"A pretty nasty experience, I guess."

"I'll say!" said the girl, shuddering at the memory.

"Do you feel up to telling me what happened?"

"Well, I live with my boyfriend in a small new apartment building on Via Ravanusella. Do you know where it is?"

"Yes, on the outskirts of town, on the way to Montelusa."

"Exactly. I was driving home alone after going to the cinema with a girlfriend, since my boyfriend didn't want to come. It was just past midnight. The last stretch of road is pretty deserted. At one point, up ahead of me I saw in my headlights a car stopped by the side of the road with its bonnet raised. There was a man tinkering with the engine, and he looked up and gestured for me to stop. Which I did instinctively. But the man immediately came up to the car, pointing a gun at the window, and ordered me to get out. As soon as I did, he told me to turn around and then violently pressed a pad soaked with chloroform over my face. I woke up two hours later, somewhere just outside Montelusa. So I called up my boyfriend and told him to come and get me. He'd been searching desperately for me for the past couple of hours, after finding my car beside the road with the door open and no one inside. But I was OK. Nobody did anything to me physically, no violence, not even a bruise or a scratch. And nothing was stolen, either."

"So, as I seem to have gathered, you got a good look at the man."

"Yes, but I couldn't describe him to you."

"Why not?"

"Because he had a cap on his head pulled all the way down over his forehead and was wearing dark glasses and a scarf covering his mouth and chin."

"Now think hard before answering. Did he seem to you like a young man or an older man?"

"But I just said . . ."

"I'm sorry, but normally a woman gets a sense of these things by instinct. Just try thinking back on those moments . . ."

The girl furrowed her brow and searched her memory. "He was an older man," she finally said with assurance. "The way he walked up to me, I'd say he didn't have the gait of a young man."

"Excellent. And when he pulled you towards him to chloroform you, did you smell anything in particular? Like cologne or aftershave?"

This time she answered readily.

"No, I got a whiff of sour perspiration. The guy seemed to sweat like a pig. And it was even cold outside, though it's only September."

"Let's continue. You were apparently the victim of an overnight kidnapping. And you're probably asking yourself a lot of questions about it. Have you formed any opinion of who it could have been and why he might have done it?"

"What do you think? Of course I have a lot of questions! Especially because I've been unable to come up with a single answer."

"Could it have been a former lover trying to take revenge?"

"What kind of revenge is that? He didn't do anything to me. If somebody wanted revenge they would have tried to rape me or knock me around."

Made perfect sense.

"What kind of job do you have at the Banca di Credito?"

"I was hired just three months ago. For now I'm the manager's secretary."

"Where did you work before that?"

"In a notary's office."

"I have no further questions," Montalbano said, standing up.

They shook hands. The young woman went out and Enzo came in.

"What do you think, Inspector?"

"I don't think it's anything directly personal against your niece or her father. There's just some nutcase out there going around kidnapping young women and fortunately not harming them. Don't worry, we'll catch him."

But, deep down, he wasn't really so sure.

Since he'd stayed late at Enzo's, the inspector decided to skip his usual walk along the jetty and go straight back to the station.

"Ahh, Chief, Mr Pitruzzo jess called, the same Pitruzzo 'at was lookin' f' yiz poissonally in poisson 'iss morning, an' 'e tanks yiz fer takin' 'im to the haspital, an' 'e says 'at seein' as how 'is 'ead don't feel so good, 'e can't come in but 'e'll come by tomorrow at ten, 'im bein' 'im, meanin' Mr Pitruzzo."

So Pitruzzo was the man Adelina bashed in the head with the frying pan.

"OK. Now get me Augello and Fazio."

He went into his office, and when the other two arrived, he told them about the latest lightning-quick, consequence-free kidnapping of another young woman.

"The two episodes have only one thing in common," he concluded.

"Both girls work at a bank," Augello and Fazio said together, almost in unison.

"Right. But I don't think we're looking at someone who was denied a loan, or anything like that."

"Why do you rule that out?" asked Augello.

"Why the hell would someone like that give a shit about a cashier or some little secretary? You want to take revenge, you plant a bomb and good night."

Silence fell.

"At what time is Manuela Smerca coming?" Montalbano then asked.

"At five," Fazio replied.

"So let's meet here in an hour. I want you both present."

Manuela didn't feel the least bit intimidated to find herself in a room at a police station together with Montalbano and his two assistants.

She was beautiful and knew it, and was also confident that she could always defend herself with her looks.

24

Indeed, when she sat down she made sure to leave her long, perfect legs in full view, and the three men couldn't help but look at them spellbound.

It was the inspector who, with a quiet sigh and a twinge of regret, broke the spell.

"Your father has already told us, in a general way, about your brief kidnapping. But I unfortunately have to ask you some more detailed questions that will force you to relive those unpleasant moments. Is that all right with you?"

"Yes, please go ahead."

"At what time were you assaulted?"

"The circle line takes about twenty minutes to get to the stop where I get off. Let's say it was a little before seven."

"So there was still plenty of daylight. The assailant was running a big risk."

"I suppose so, but I don't think it was really all that risky. The road is very straight there, and you can see cars or people coming from far away. But it is pretty rare to see other cars or people along the road."

"Did you get a look at the man's licence-plate number?"

"No, I forgot to look."

"What kind of car was it?"

"I couldn't say."

"What colour?"

"Dark."

Why, after all, would she have paid such close attention to a car stopped at the side of the road?

"Your father said you weren't able to get a good look at the man's face. Is that so?"

"Yes, I can confirm that."

"When he was pressing the pad with the chloroform against your face, I imagine the assailant held you against his body and —"

"Yes, he was holding me tight, pressing my body against his."

"Did you notice any kind of smell? More precisely —"

"I see exactly what you're getting at. Yes, he smelled bad, as if he was sweating profusely."

"And as he was squeezing you, could you tell whether he was sexually aroused?"

The question elicited a broad smile from Manuela. "No, he wasn't at all aroused. On the contrary."

"What do you mean?"

"I think he was afraid."

"Of what?"

"Of what he was doing."

"So he was afraid of getting caught?"

"That, too. But I had the feeling — though I couldn't really tell you why — that he was scared by his own actions."

A kidnapper afraid to kidnap? Now that was a new twist!

CHAPTER
THREE

"Are you telling me he seemed reluctant to do what he was doing?" Montalbano asked with surprise.

"I could be mistaken, but that was the feeling I got. He wasn't rough and wasn't even terribly aggressive. He was just as forceful as he needed to be."

Smart girl.

"Did he seem young to you, or more like an older man?"

"Definitely an older man."

"Do you have any explanation for what happened?"

"I've been lying awake for several nights now, I assure you, and I still haven't been able to come up with a plausible explanation."

"Are you married or engaged?"

"No. I don't even have a steady boyfriend."

"Well, attractive as you are, you must have many suitors."

"Thanks. I can't complain, I guess."

"Could it have been a rejected suitor?"

"I was lying there lifeless, at his complete disposal, and he didn't take advantage of me. So, I don't think so."

"Is there anything else you can tell me?"

"No, not really. He didn't undo a single button on me, and he didn't even search through my handbag."

"How can you really tell?"

"I always keep my things in a specific order in there, and when I opened it to get my phone, I could see that everything was in its proper place, even though I was a bit dazed."

"Did you know that just the day before, there'd been another overnight kidnapping exactly like yours?"

"Really?!" the young woman said in astonishment.

Then, after thinking about it for a moment, she asked the most logical question possible: "Did she look like me?"

"Not in the least. The other woman had dark curly hair and was rather petite . . . But, like you, she worked in a bank."

Manuela was silently thoughtful for a moment. Then she said:

"If I were you I wouldn't lend too much weight to the fact that we both work in banks. It has to be a coincidence."

"Why?"

"If they really wanted to hurt the banks they would have done something else. This doesn't make any sense. But . . . have you been able to establish that the assailant was the same in both cases?" she asked.

It was an intelligent question. "Yes, it was the same person."

The girl threw up her hands. "I don't know what to say."

After Manuela left, Montalbano, Augello, and Fazio sat there in silence, staring at each other.

Nothing about this whole affair made any sense. As the girl herself had said.

"Maybe he's some kind of maniac who gets off on hugging women after they've lost consciousness," Augello ventured.

But he said it in the tone of someone who doesn't really believe what he's saying. And so he immediately formulated another hypothesis. "Or maybe he photographs them in strange poses."

"There's one thing I'm sure of," said Fazio, "which is that there will be more assaults."

"I agree," said Montalbano. "But there was something Manuela said that really intrigued me, something she was quite insistent about, which is that the assailant was frightened by what he was doing."

"Explain," said Augello.

"The fact that he was afraid tells me at least two things: first that the assailant is new to this kind of thing — he's a beginner, and so we can rule out him being some sort of pro with a whole organization behind him. In all likelihood he's acting alone. The second thing is that he's in some kind of situation where he's forced to commit lightning-quick kidnappings."

"Do you mean for a third party? That other people are forcing him to kidnap these girls?"

"Maybe. But it might also be a situation where he did something and is now in a position where, for whatever reason, he's forced to kidnap young women. In short, these kidnappings might be just red herrings."

"So, what are we going to do?" asked Fazio.

"I haven't the slightest idea," replied the inspector. They sat there a few moments in silence, meditating on their powerlessness and inability to make any sense of these apparently senseless acts.

As the passing minutes began to weigh heavier and heavier, Montalbano broke the silence.

"Still, despite the fog we're in, we do have one point in our favour," he said.

Augello and Fazio surfaced from the depths of their thoughts and focused their attention.

"So far none of the newsmen in town knows anything about these kidnappings, and the gossips haven't found out yet, either."

"Why do you consider that a point in our favour?" asked Augello.

"It's possible the attacker was hoping to create a big stir with his kidnappings. Maybe the silence will disappoint him and lead him to do something more drastic to provoke a reaction."

"You mean something like a third kidnapping, but this time one that lasts several days and forces the family to make a public appeal for our help?" asked Fazio.

"Something like that. And, if so, I hope that in so doing he'll make a false move."

He feasted on Adelina's *pasta 'ncasciata* out on the veranda.

Every so often, as he was eating, the thought of the two kidnappings would pop into his head, and he would banish it at once.

He had nothing at hand to go on, and so it would have been pointless, and possibly even counterproductive, to speculate idly.

When he'd finished eating, he phoned Livia in Boccadasse.

At a certain point in their conversation she asked him what he was working on, and Montalbano told her about the two young women who had been kidnapped.

Livia remained silent for a moment, then spoke. "Something similar happened once in Genoa, a very long time ago. I was still in school."

"Tell me about it."

"I don't remember much. The guy who did it was impotent, and he could only get aroused by sniffing women's panties, which he was able to do by rendering his victims unconscious."

"He would take them off the women?"

"No, he left them on them."

"I don't think my case is the same."

"Why not?"

"I don't know. Just a feeling."

"Well, no offence, Salvo, but your instinct is not what it was, say, thirty years ago."

This reference to his age upset him, but he realized, deep down, that Livia was right.

Why not follow her advice as well? Dismissing the idea of a maniac out of hand might prove to be a big mistake.

He slept well that night, and therefore arrived at work the following morning sharp and elegant, fresh and well rested. The skin around his eye was turning light blue, and his ear was only about half as swollen as the day before.

"Call Fazio and tell him —" he started saying to Catarella upon entering.

"He in't onna premisses, Chief."

"Where is he?"

"'Ere was a larcenous fire at a store lass night, an' so 'e went to the scene o' the crime."

"Then get me Inspector Augello."

"'E in't onna premisses, neither, Chief."

"And where'd he go?"

"'E called sayin' as how 'e — meanin' 'im, Isspector Augello — 'ad to take 'is son — 'is own son bein' 'is, I mean — to the haspital 'cause 'e hoit 'is leg."

Montalbano felt horrified.

This meant that he would have no choice but to spend the morning signing papers, those hated papers piled up in precarious stacks on his desk.

If it had been up to him, all such documents would remain "outstanding" for the rest of eternity.

He went into his office, sat down in the small armchair, cursed for five minutes without interruption, then took the first document, signed it, then grabbed another. After he'd been at it for a good while, the telephone rang.

"Chief, 'at'd be the poisson of Mr Pitruzzo, poissonally in poisson."

The inspector looked at his watch: ten minutes to nine.

But wasn't he supposed to come at ten?

"Show him into my office."

He would have been willing to receive even the devil in person, just to stop signing papers.

Pitruzzo came in, they shook hands and smiled, and the inspector sat him down.

"How's your head?"

"Much better, thanks. I apologize for not coming yesterday, as promised, but I didn't feel up to going out. I preferred to stay at home, and I think it did me a world of good."

"So, what can I do for you, Mr Pitruzzo?"

The man smiled.

"Virduzzo's the name, Alfredo Virduzzo."

Montalbano cursed under his breath. Why had he trusted Catarella yet again, when he was constitutionally incapable of getting anyone's name right? Why did he always fall for it?

"I beg your pardon. So, please tell me."

"You should know that I —"

The outside phone line rang.

"Excuse me just a moment," said Montalbano, picking up the receiver.

It was Fazio.

"I'm sorry, Chief, but it's probably best you come here yourself."

"Why, are there complications?" asked the inspector, keeping things vague in the presence of a stranger.

"Yeah."

"Something that'll take a while?"

"Yeah."

"Give me the address, and I'll be right there."

Via dei Fiori, number 38. He'd never heard of that street before. He stood up, and Virduzzo did the same.

"I'm terribly sorry, but . . ."

How many polite apologies had the two men already exchanged that morning? You'd think they were Chinese or something.

"I understand," Virduzzo said in resignation.

Montalbano threw him a sop.

"If you want, you could come back late this afternoon . . ."

"Would six p.m. be all right?" Virduzzo asked hopefully.

"It's fine with me."

Not trusting Catarella, he called Fazio back and had him explain how to find the street. It wasn't far away. A twenty-minute walk and he'd be right there.

Naturally, in Via dei Fiori there wasn't a flower to be seen for love or money.

The street was in a neighbourhood of old, deteriorated buildings that the commune had decided to renovate to create what one might call an "artists' quarter".

There was one painter's studio, three photographers' studios, two galleries exhibiting paintings and sculptures that nobody bought, a few houses with creatively painted facades, and a so-called Caffè degli Artisti.

At number 38 was a small two-storey building. The front door was open, and outside it stood a municipal policeman, who immediately recognized the inspector and stood aside to let him in after greeting him.

Montalbano returned the greeting and went inside.

Opposite the entranceway, a bit to the left, were the remains of a wooden door consumed by fire; to the right was a staircase with an elegant banister that led upstairs and didn't look too damaged.

Montalbano went through the charred door and found himself in a large shop that sold televisions, mobile phones, and other electronic stuff.

He'd come through the back door; the main entrance for the clientele, flanked by a display window, was at the opposite end and gave onto the main street of the neighbourhood.

The rolling metal shutters had been lowered halfway both for the entrance and the display window, letting a bit of light in; otherwise, the interior would have been in pitch-darkness, further darkened by the veil of soot covering everything.

"Fazio!" he cried out. No reply.

He decided there was nothing to be done in there. Possibly also because there was a dense, acrid odour that brought tears to his eyes and made him cough. He turned around and went out.

At just that moment he saw Fazio coming in through the main door.

"The policeman came and told me you were here."

"Where were you?"

"In a bar nearby. My throat was all dry from the soot and I couldn't breathe."

"Why did you ask me to come?"

"Chief, I would never have troubled you if there wasn't a problem. Let's go upstairs, it'll be easier to talk."

Fazio led the way. The door was open, and they went in.

The apartment, to judge from the entrance, must have been nicely furnished.

"This is where the owner lives. His name is Marcello Di Carlo."

"Where is he?"

Fazio seemed not to have heard the question. "Want me to show you the apartment?" he asked.

If Fazio was acting this way, there must be a reason. Montalbano nodded in assent.

Fazio led the way. The front door was open, and they went in.

The vestibule area led to a corridor with doors on both sides.

Dining room, living room, ultramodern kitchen, bathroom with Jacuzzi on the right; master bedroom, bathroom, another large bedroom, and a study on the left.

It was all clean and in perfect order, but gave the impression that no one had been living there for a while.

They went back into the vestibule and sat down. In the short time he'd been in the place, Montalbano had already formed a precise opinion.

"I get it," he said. "There's no sign of this Di Carlo."

"Exactly."

"Any idea how old he is?"

"About forty."

"Married?"

"No."

"Any relatives?"

"Yes, a sister, Daniela, who is married and lives in Montelusa. Or so I was told at the bar, where Di Carlo is a regular customer."

"We have to try and find out her married name so we can call her."

"Already taken care of," said Fazio.

It always got terribly on Montalbano's nerves when Fazio uttered those four words.

But this time he managed to control himself.

"The husband's name is Ingrassia, and I was able to talk to him on the phone."

"And what did he say?"

"He seemed more concerned with the fire than with his brother-in-law."

"What do you mean?"

"He said Marcello is a good-looking guy who likes to enjoy life. He spent the whole of August in Lanzarote, from where he called his sister and told her it was a sort of honeymoon. Apparently he'd found someone. He got back in touch on the thirty-first of the month, telling her he was back in Vigàta, but since then Daniela has had no news of him. She thinks he maybe brought the girl back from Lanzarote with him and is now taking her around and showing her all the sights of our beautiful island."

"I'm sorry, but who's looking after the shop while he is enjoying the company of his latest girlfriend?"

"There's a salesman by the name of Filippo Caruana, who's got the keys. He's down in the bar right now, if you want to talk to him."

"And what did Daniela say about the fire?"

"She immediately said it was the Mafia. Without any hesitation. Back in July her brother told her they'd raised the protection fee and he had no intention of paying it."

Montalbano sat there thinking.

"Go and get me the salesman," he said a moment later.

Fazio went out and came back five minutes later with a lad of about twenty with an intelligent face.

"I would like you to tell me whether you noticed anything unusual in Di Carlo's behaviour when he returned from his holiday."

The youth replied at once.

"Well, moodwise, he was more cheerful than usual."

"Did you get any sense of the reason for the change?"

"He told me himself, the first day we reopened the shop."

"And what was that?"

"He'd fallen in love."

"During his holiday in the Canary Islands?"

"No, apparently they'd met here in Vigàta in early June and immediately hit it off. By chance she had reserved a place in Tenerife for July and August, and he'd reserved in Lanzarote just for August. So on the first of August he went to get her in Tenerife and brought her back to Lanzarote with him."

"I see. And did they come back together?"

"I can't really say with any certainty, but I think so. Di Carlo told me he'd be back on the thirty-first of August."

"What makes you think they came back together?"

"The fact that his habits changed."

"How?"

"The shop closes every evening at eight p.m. Ever since he's been back, he leaves at six-thirty. So now I'm the one who takes care of closing up."

"And are you always the one who opens up in the morning?"

"No, he usually is. But in the last three days I've found the shutters down when I got to work, so I've had to open them myself."

"And at what time has he come in?"

"He hasn't come in at all. I haven't seen him for three days. He hasn't even phoned."

"Has he by any chance said anything about the woman he spent his holiday with?"

"Like what?"

"Name, where she's from, stuff like that . . ."

"He didn't say any more than I've already told you."

"Did he show you a picture of her?"

"No."

"Has he ever been absent for several days like this in the past?"

"Yes. But he acted differently."

"Meaning?"

"Meaning, he told me where he was going and how long he would be away."

"Does Di Carlo have a mobile phone?"

"Of course."

"Have you tried calling him?"

"Naturally. But it's always turned off. I've even sent him text messages, but haven't had any replies."

"How has the shop been doing?"

"Pretty well, actually, considering the economic crisis."

"Do you know if he has anyone who cleans his apartment?"

"A woman comes every other day. But I can't —"

"The people at the bar gave me her name and phone number," said Fazio. "They know her, too, since she used to clean for them as well."

"What kind of car does he own?"

The youth opened his mouth but didn't have time to say anything before Fazio spoke.

"A Porsche Cayenne."

"And where does he keep this treasure?"

"In a parking garage two blocks from here."

CHAPTER
FOUR

It was of the utmost importance to find out whether the car was there or not, to have any sense at all of Di Carlo's movements.

"We'll have to go and see whether —"

"Already taken care of," said Fazio.

"Ohhhhhhhh!" Montalbano exploded, unable to control himself this time.

It had come out as a kind of very loud, wolflike howl that scared the hell out of the other two.

"Are you feeling all right, Chief?" Fazio asked with concern.

"Yeah, it's nothing . . . Just this rheumatic pain that sometimes creeps up on me . . . So, you were saying?"

"I was about to say that the car's not there. Di Carlo came and took it one afternoon a few days ago, but they don't know exactly when, and he hasn't brought it back since. I have the licence-plate number."

Montalbano didn't have any more questions to ask the youth, so he dismissed him.

"But," he said before the young man was out the door, "if you get any news of Di Carlo, directly or indirectly, please let us know immediately."

The young man said goodbye and went out.

"What do you think?" asked Fazio.

"He may just be out tooling around with his girlfriend, and then again he may not be. If he's not out tooling around, then, sooner or later, she will come forward to ask us for news of her missing boyfriend. What did the firemen say?"

"That it was a clear case of arson."

"How was it done?"

"Somebody came through the front door with a skeleton key, then opened the back door of the store with another skeleton key. Then, once inside, they emptied two jerry cans of petrol, lit a match, and left."

"So, from what I can gather, they were trying to make as little noise as possible."

"So it seems."

"Maybe they thought Di Carlo was at home sleeping."

"Maybe."

"Tell me something: who opened the door to the apartment?"

"I found it already open."

"So was it the firemen?"

"I don't know."

"Who's the fire chief?"

"Guggino."

"Give him a call and ask him about the door."

As Fazio was phoning, Montalbano got up and started pacing about, smoking a cigarette. When he saw that Fazio had finished, he sat back down.

"Guggino says that the door was already open when they got there, too, and there was nobody inside."

"That changes the picture a little," the inspector observed.

"What do you mean?"

"Well, it certainly wasn't Di Carlo, the owner, who left the door open."

"It could have been the cleaning lady."

"Give her a ring and find out what her hours are."

The conversation was a quick one.

"The cleaning lady says she only comes here in the morning, but hasn't been here for the past week because she's been really ill with the flu."

"So the cleaning lady had nothing to do with it. Which leaves us with two possibilities: either there's no connection between the fire and Di Carlo's disappearance, or there is a connection, and a very close one."

"So you're saying that, in the second case, whoever set fire to the store also kidnapped Di Carlo?"

"Exactly."

Fazio looked doubtful.

"I'm sorry, but this isn't at all the way the Mafia usually operate!"

"You're absolutely right. It's not the way they usually operate. And that's got me very worried."

"What should we do?"

"I want to see the study."

The room wasn't very big, but enough to fit a white, semi-circular, and very modern desk that looked like a cross between a missile and a Formula One car; behind it was an aerodynamic, adjustable swivel armchair with so many levers and switches that one probably needed to get a licence before sitting down in it; and in front of it were two normal chairs. The wall opposite the desk was entirely covered by a huge bookcase with very few books but, to make up for it, cluttered with knickknacks such as seashells, little animals made of terracotta and glass, miniature houses, and a few exotic musical instruments. Probably travel souvenirs.

Also of note were four cameras. Built into the wall on the right was a large filing cabinet, which the inspector opened. You really couldn't say that Di Carlo was a disorderly man. Neatly filed away, each with its own binder, were correspondences with suppliers, invoices, receipts, and suchlike.

Montalbano sat carefully down in the armchair and opened the left-hand drawer in the desk. More business-related documents. Then he opened the right-hand drawer. It was full of photo albums. Apparently Di Carlo aspired to be a great landscape photographer, since that was the most prevalent subject.

"Two things are missing," the inspector observed.

"One is the computer," said Fazio. "What's the other?"

"Photos of the girl he was with. With someone as obsessed with photos as this guy, you can imagine how many he must have taken of her."

"You're right."

"I'm sure he took the computer with him, or else, if he was kidnapped, they took the computer, too. But where are the photos?"

He got up.

"You know what I say? Let's go back to the station. There's nothing else to see here."

44

"If you don't mind, I'm going to use the bathroom for a minute," said Fazio.

He went out, and moments later the inspector heard him calling him.

Fazio had opened the curtain in the shower.

On the floor were two large yellow bags, one empty and the other full to bursting, a box of kitchen matches, and a great deal of black ash all around the shower drain.

The inspector bent down, picked up the swollen bag, and opened it. Photos of pretty young women, clothed, in swimming costumes, and naked.

"Looks like our friend Di Carlo was getting rid of his souvenirs of past loves," he said.

There were at least some ten photos for each girl, which Di Carlo, with customary care, had not only grouped together in a stack held together by a rubber band but, on the back of the last photo in each stack, had also written the girl's name and the dates of the duration of their time together.

There were sixteen stacks in all. The first featured Adele (13 January to 22 April 2010) and the last, Giovanna (3 March to 30 March 2012). But the upshot was that there were still no photos of the girl he had gone to Lanzarote to see and was still with.

"This Di Carlo's love affairs certainly never lasted very long," Fazio observed.

"That's true, but apparently it's different now, with the new girl," said Montalbano.

"How do you know that?"

"I know it from the fact that he wanted to burn all the photos of his other women. He wanted to, that is. But apparently he never managed to do so. And this definitely means something."

"Namely?"

"Namely that Di Carlo hasn't yet brought his new girlfriend here, since his plan to destroy the traces of his old affairs wasn't completed, and so, for now, he sleeps at her place. Logically we can surmise that the girl has her own place, since I don't think they're always sleeping in hotels."

"What should we do with these photos?"

"Leave them where we found them."

Exiting the bathroom, they were walking down the hall when they heard a woman's voice call from the stairwell.

"Mr Fazio!"

"Who's that?" asked Montalbano.

"I have no idea. I'll go and look."

The inspector waited in the hallway. Fazio returned. "It's Daniela Ingrassia, Di Carlo's sister. She's come down from Montelusa and wants to talk to you. Will you see her here, or should I tell her to come in to the station?"

"I'll talk to her here."

After exchanging introductions, they sat down in the vestibule.

Signora Daniela was a nice-looking, well-dressed brunette somewhere in her mid-thirties.

She made no effort to hide her agitation and was worrying a little handkerchief to death with her hands.

Since nobody seemed ready to open the conversation, she spoke first.

"Forgive me for barging in on you like this, but I went to the police station and they told me you were here, and so I . . ."

"You did the right thing," said the inspector.

"Have you by any chance had any news of Marcello in the meantime?" she asked anxiously.

"Not yet."

Daniela's face darkened further.

"I would like to explain . . . I don't know where to begin . . . When Mr Fazio called me I didn't realize at first how serious this all was . . . Then, after I started thinking about it . . ."

"What made you change your mind?"

"Well, some time in late June Marcello came to our house for dinner. He was different from his usual cheerful self, and I asked him why. He didn't want to tell me, but by the end of the meal he decided to. He was worried because there had been a serious drop in sales at his shop and, as if this wasn't enough, he'd been told his protection fee had doubled. And he told us he wasn't going to pay it. He came back to our place for dinner just before going away on holiday. On that occasion he told us he'd met a fantastic new woman, but he also told us he hadn't paid the protection money and as a result he'd been getting some very threatening phone calls."

"What did they threaten him with?"

"Torching his car, burning down his shop . . ."

"Did they also threaten to kidnap him?"

"He didn't say so to me."

"And when he returned from his holiday, you only spoke to him by phone?"

"Yes. We didn't get together."

"How did he seem to you?"

"He was, well . . . euphoric, that's the word. He'd just spent a month of bliss, he told me. And he added that things were serious with this girl, very serious. He even led me to think they might get married. I was honestly quite happy he seemed to be settling down. I told him I wanted to meet her, and he replied that he had no problem with that, and that one of these evenings he would bring her over for dinner."

"Did he tell you the girl's name?"

"No."

"Did he say where she lived?"

"Yes, he said she lived here in Vigàta, but I didn't ask him for anything more specific."

"Did he say whether she had a job?"

"No."

"Did he mention again the protection payment and the problems with the shop?"

"Not at all . . . It was as if he was still in Lanzarote with his girlfriend. As if he was still on holiday. He hadn't had time yet to readjust to the real world."

"Do you know any of your brother's friends?"

"He's got quite a few . . . The first one who comes to mind is Giorgio Bonfiglio. He's his closest friend."

"Do you know where he lives?"

"No, but you'll find him in the phone book. I talked to him just before coming here."

"You talked to Bonfiglio?"

"Yes. I told him everything I knew. He hadn't heard from Marcello for days either. And that really troubles me. It makes me very anxious. I'm worried they may have hurt him. Inspector, I beg you, please do everything you can because —"

"There's a slight problem, signora. Your brother is a legal adult. It's quite possible he decided to disappear of his own free will . . ."

"I don't think so."

"I don't, either, but for the moment I'm stuck. I can only act if a family member files a special report."

"I see," said Daniela.

It was clear that she didn't know whether or not to file the report. The inspector helped her out a little.

"Talk it over with your husband. If you decide to do it, call police headquarters and ask for Mr Fazio."

Daniela stood up, thanked them both, said goodbye, and went out.

"I'm starting to have my doubts," said Fazio.

"About what?"

"What if it was Marcello himself who set fire to his shop, hoping the blame would fall on the Mafia? We know from his sister that business was bad and the protection fee had been doubled. This way he gets the insurance money, and a good night to all. Also, just to complicate matters, he sets up the little drama of his front door being left open and him completely vanished."

"That could be a viable hypothesis," said the inspector. "But in the meantime let's try to find out as much as we can about Marcello Di Carlo. We'll go back to the office now, and I want you to ring Bonfiglio right away and summon him to the station for four o'clock."

"Any news, Cat?"

"Nah, Chief."

"Has Inspector Augello returned?"

"'E's jess back now, Chief."

"Tell him to come to my office."

He'd barely sat down when Mimì walked in.

"Wha'd your kid do to his leg?"

"Nothing, idiot."

"So why did it take you so long?"

"Actually I got back a good two hours ago, but I had to go out again immediately."

"Why, what happened?"

"A car was torched last night. And since I'd taken a report for a stolen car, I wanted to check it out. I believe I mentioned that theft to you."

"Yeah, I vaguely remember."

"The man reporting the theft was the car's owner, an engineer by the name of Cosimato. It was a special model of Mitsubishi, with an extra-large boot."

Montalbano twisted in his armchair and huffed. "Listen, Mimì, you're just boring me. I don't care about stolen cars."

"Well, in the present case you're making a big mistake."

"Oh, yeah?"

"Yeah," said Mimì, glaring at him defiantly.

"All right, then, go on."

50

"Well, the car turns out to be none other than Cosimato's Mitsubishi. So I'd guessed right. But whoever set it on fire did a poor job of it, since the rear of the vehicle remained almost intact. So I opened the boot and immediately saw something strange."

"Namely?"

"A metal ring covered with fabric, of the kind that women use to gather their hair. This got me thinking: maybe the guy going around kidnapping young women had used this car . . ."

"So what did you do?"

"I did what I was supposed to do. I called up the Forensics lab, waited for them to arrive on the scene, and then I came back here."

"And how did you leave it with them?"

"They're going to call me this afternoon."

"Mimì, you have no idea how much effort it costs me to say this to you, but I'll say it anyway: very well done. You've really —"

"Wait, stop right there! Otherwise the effort might be so tremendous you'll end up with a hernia."

As soon as the inspector sat down, Enzo came over to take his order.

It was early, and aside from the inspector, there were no other customers, so they could talk openly.

"Shall I bring you a few antipasti as usual?"

"Yes, but you have to do me a favour while I'm eating them."

"Whatever you say."

"Call your niece and ask her if she lost anything during her kidnapping."

"What do you mean?"

"The kidnapper stuffed her into his boot, didn't he? And even if he did it carefully, trying not to harm her, it's still an act of physical force, so it's possible your niece lost something in the process — I dunno, an earring, bracelet, something like that."

Enzo returned as Montalbano was finishing his antipasti. "My niece lost a little ring of no value that she was very fond of. It was too big for her. But in all honesty she doesn't know exactly when she lost it. Have there been any new developments?"

"Nothing yet."

After leaving the trattoria he took his customary stroll along the jetty, out to the flat rock just under the lighthouse.

He sat down on the rock, lit a cigarette, and started thinking.

Even if Mimì Augello was right, this didn't mean with any certainty that there would be no more overnight kidnappings.

It was possible the kidnapper had stolen another car in the fear that the one he'd been using might be identified.

But it was also possible that the kidnapper had no further intention or need to conduct any more kidnappings.

In both cases, however, the main question still remained unanswered. And this was: what was the purpose of the kidnappings?

None of it seemed to make any sense.

And yet there had to be an explanation for it all.

"Think you could help me find it?" he asked a crab who was staring at him from the lower end of the rock.

The crab did not reply.

"Thanks just the same," said Montalbano.

Then he sighed, stood up, started walking slowly, one lazy step at a time, back to his car.

Just a few minutes before four, Fazio knocked and came into the inspector's office.

"Do you want me here when you talk to Bonfiglio?"

"Yes, have a seat. In the meantime I can tell you what Augello has discovered."

He told him about the car that had been torched and the circlet. Before Fazio could venture a comment, the phone rang.

"Ahh, Chief, 'ere's a Mr Bongiglio 'ere poissonally in poisson, an' 'e says you summonsed 'im 'ere yisself."

"Yes, that's right, send him in."

As soon as Giorgio Bonfiglio appeared, Montalbano and Fazio exchanged a questioning glance.

Since Daniela had described him as Marcello's closest friend, they were expecting someone of about the same age, around forty. Whereas the man before them looked about sixty, but was well groomed in his person and attire.

Montalbano asked him to take a seat. Bonfiglio sat down on the edge of the chair, clearly ill at ease.

The inspector went straight to the matter at hand, with a question that took them both by surprise:

"Are you married?"

"Why do you want to know?" the man asked, a bit flabbergasted.

"Please answer my question."

"Marriage has never even crossed my mind. I'm the sort of man who's usually called an unapologetic bachelor."

"How did you become friends with Marcello Di Carlo?"

"We met about ten years ago at a dinner party at the house of some friends we had in common. We immediately took a liking to each other, and so, despite the difference in age, we became friends."

"Does Di Carlo confide in you?"

Bonfiglio smiled and puffed himself up in pride.

CHAPTER
FIVE

The inspector became irritated.

"Please express yourself verbally, if you don't mind."

"Of course he confides in me. Since I'm older than him, I sort of became his confessor and adviser."

"Do you think he tells you everything?"

"Well, I don't know . . . Let's say almost everything."

"Did he tell you that the Mafia doubled his protection fee?"

"Of course."

"Could you tell me what kind of advice you gave him about that?"

Bonfiglio didn't hesitate.

"I told him to pay. Without any fuss. But as far as I can tell, Marcello seems to have held firm in his refusal to pay."

"Why did you tell him to pay?"

"Forgive me for speaking frankly, and please understand that I do not mean to offend anyone. I told him to pay because, in the first place, you guys — meaning you the police and the carabinieri — are powerless to do anything about the protection racket."

He stopped, expecting some kind of reaction from Montalbano, which never came. The inspector merely asked:

"And in the second place?"

"In the second place, I pointed out to him that it wasn't really a doubling of the amount, but just a mild increase. He retorted that, taking into consideration his drop in revenues, the increase, in percentage terms, came to twice what it was before. And from his perspective, he was right."

"So what I think you're saying is that you're of the opinion that both the fire at the electronics shop and your friend's disappearance are the work of the Mafia, because he refused to make his payment."

Bonfiglio threw up his hands.

"That seems like the most logical conclusion, don't you think? Marcello told me that all the shop owners in the area had been presented with an increase in protection fees, and that many had said they wouldn't pay. I'm convinced that after the fire and Marcello's disappearance, all the others will pay up, just to be safe."

"So do you think that Marcello will be released sooner or later?"

Bonfiglio's face darkened.

"I honestly don't know the answer to that question."

"Just try."

"My heart tells me yes, but my brain tells me no."

"Let's move on. Do you remember when was the last time you saw Di Carlo?"

"Yes, that I can tell you precisely. It was two days before he left for his holiday, and therefore July the twenty-ninth, at which time he told me he would be back on August the thirty-first, in the afternoon."

"So you didn't meet him after he got back?"

"No."

"Why not?"

"I wasn't in Vigàta, I was in Palermo. I got back just the day before yesterday."

"For business?"

"I went to help my sister, who is gravely ill. My brother-in-law was abroad on a military mission, and she was by herself."

"Did you and Di Carlo talk on the phone during this time?"

"Yes, we did. We spoke three times."

"Did he tell you he'd fallen in love?"

Bonfiglio smiled.

"Actually, he'd called me from Lanzarote to tell me. And he repeated it to me the last time we spoke, though adding the bit about it being a serious thing, this time."

Bonfiglio's smile broadened.

"Do you find that amusing?"

"Well, frankly, yes."

"Why?"

"It's the fourth time in ten years that I've heard him say 'this time it's really serious'. The best part is that he actually believes it. He starts imagining his future life with the girl — marriage, raising a family . . . It's like some kind of disease that puts him into a fever for a few months, then, suddenly, from one day to the next, he's cured . . ."

"Did he tell you the girl's name?"

"No. The other times he not only told me their first names, but also their last names, age, address, physical features, good points, bad points, tastes, everything. But, this time, nothing."

"Didn't that seem strange to you?"

"Of course. So strange that I asked several times why he was so reluctant to talk about her."

"And what did he say?"

"He just said he would tell me when he got back, and that it would be a big surprise for me."

"And how did you interpret that statement?"

"There's only one way to interpret it, which is that it's someone I know."

"Any idea who it might be?"

"No, not really."

"Why not?"

"I've been with too many women these past ten years to remember them all. As I said, I'm an unapologetic bachelor."

"I'm sorry, but what do you do for a living?"

"I'm the exclusive representative of a number of world-famous jewellers."

"Pays well?"

"I can't complain."

"Speaking of which, I got the impression that Di Carlo lives a life somewhat beyond his means. Am I mistaken?"

"No, you're not mistaken."

"Does he have debts, as far as you know?"

Bonfiglio hesitated for a moment before answering. "A few."

"With banks?"

"Yes."

"Only with banks?"

"Not only."

"Do you mean to say that he has turned to loan sharks for money?"

"Unfortunately, yes."

"Has he ever asked you to lend him money?"

"Yes."

"And did you agree?"

"Yes."

"Considerable sums?"

Bonfiglio seemed embarrassed, then spoke. "I'd rather not answer that."

"And did he pay you back?"

"In part."

He was clearly lying.

"I've no further questions," said the inspector, standing up. "Naturally, if your friend Marcello gets in touch with you, you must let us know at once."

They shook hands, and Bonfiglio went out.

"This confirms my suspicion," said Fazio.

"Explain."

"Bonfiglio told us the guy was riddled with debts. He burned down his shop for the insurance money. And in my opinion he has not been kidnapped. He's gone and hidden somewhere and will reappear in a few days, all fresh and smiling, claiming he was kidnapped because he stood up to the Mafiosi."

Montalbano remained silent.

"What do you think about it?" asked Fazio.

"Your hypothesis might make sense, but on one condition: that Di Carlo has an accomplice."

"An accomplice? And who would that be?"

"The girl he's in love with."

"But it's possible he hasn't told her about any of this."

"But in that case the girl would have come and reported him missing, don't you think?"

"Yeah, you're right," said Fazio, disappointed. "Still, I don't know why, but I get the feeling this story is more complicated than it appears."

"I agree," said Montalbano.

At that moment Augello came in looking triumphant and holding two small cellophane bags in his hand.

"In addition to the circlet, Forensics also found a little ring in the boot of the torched car. Here they are."

He put the two small bags down on the inspector's desk. Montalbano looked at them.

"The circlet must belong to Manuela, while the little ring belongs to Enzo's niece," he said eventually.

Mimì looked at him in shock. "How do you know that?"

"Mimì, I don't have magic powers. The explanation's quite simple, really. Enzo told me today, when I went to eat at his trattoria. Now I'm going to give you an assignment that you're sure to enjoy. Take your little cellophane bags and show them to the two women. If they acknowledge the objects, it will confirm definitively that that car was used for the kidnappings."

"I'll go right now," said Augello, picking up the bags and heading for the door.

"Wait a second," said the inspector, stopping him in his tracks. "In your recent past as a whoremonger . . ."

"I never went to prostitutes," Augello objected.

"In your past life as a womanizer, then, did you ever meet a man named Giorgio Bonfiglio?"

"Absolutely!"

"Is he trustworthy?"

"If you tell me why you're so interested, I can probably give you a better answer."

Montalbano told him everything.

Mimì stood there for a moment in thoughtful silence, then spoke.

"Professionally speaking," he said, "meaning as a representative for producers of fine jewellery, I think he's beyond reproach. As a man with a long habit of bullshitting women, on the other hand, he's certainly told some pretty big lies. You should probably also know that he's a gutsy, inveterate poker player who can bluff with the best of them."

"OK, thanks."

Augello went out. Fazio looked over at Montalbano. "Assuming you feel like telling me, why did you ask him for information on Bonfiglio?"

"Remember the salesman at his shop who said that Marcello had met the girl here in Vigàta in early June?"

"Yes."

"And remember that Signora Daniela told us that her brother Marcello had spoken to her about a wonderful girl shortly thereafter?"

"Yep."

"Good. Because Bonfiglio told us he learned of the existence of this girl from a phone call Marcello made to him from Lanzarote in August. Now, think this over carefully: does it seem logical to you that Marcello would talk about this with his sister and his salesman but not with his closest friend?"

"You're right . . ."

"There are only two possible explanations. The first is that Marcello did talk to him about her but Bonfiglio, for reasons we don't know yet, has an interest in pretending he doesn't know the girl. The second possible explanation is that Marcello in fact did not talk to him about her. So the question is: why not? And here we might venture the fairly logical explanation that in revealing the girl's name Marcello would have provoked a strong reaction from his friend, and so, fearing such a reaction, Marcello has postponed it for as long as possible."

"Are you imagining some kind of violent reaction?"

"Not necessarily, but don't forget that Bonfiglio has lent Marcello money, and a tidy sum at that, which so far has only been returned in part."

"Which of your two hypotheses do you think is the more likely scenario?"

"Right off the top of my head I would say that Marcello told him about the girl in June."

The telephone rang.

62

"Chief, sorry to distoib yiz in yer affice an' all, bu' 'ere's a call onna line fer Fazio who ain't in 'is affice but in yers."

Fazio said a few things over the phone and then hung up. "That was Signora Daniela, who'd just spoken with her husband."

"And what have they decided?"

"They would rather wait two or three more days before filing a missing person's report."

"So, knowing Marcello, they're being careful. At any rate, missing person's report or not, we'll move ahead just the same."

The phone rang again.

"Chief, 'at'd be Mr Pitruzzo onna line, an'na hereto-foresaid wantsa —"

"Put him on."

Montalbano instinctively looked at his watch. It was twenty past six. Virduzzo sounded troubled.

"Inspector Montalbano, I'm sorry, but it's beginning to seem like everything is conspiring to prevent us from meeting."

"Weren't you supposed to be here at six?"

"Yes, but I won't be able to come."

"Why not?"

"Because unfortunately I had to go to Montelusa, to A&E. And there's a long wait."

"Did something happen to you?"

"Nothing new, but I'm feeling very dizzy and can no longer stand up."

The blows from Adelina's frying pan were therefore quasi-lethal.

"Shall we say tomorrow morning at nine?" Montalbano suggested.

"All right. I can't wait to talk to you. Thank you."

He hung up. It couldn't be anything important; otherwise, Virduzzo, dizzy or not, would have come.

Fazio turned to the subject of interest to him. "So, how should we proceed about Di Carlo?"

"We'll start with our usual strategy. You find out what people are saying around town. Ask as many people as you can what —"

The phone rang for the third time.

"Jesus, what now!" the inspector exclaimed, picking up the receiver.

Catarella's voice was breathless and trembling.

"Ahh, Chief, 'ere's some scary-soundin' guy's askin' f' help an' I don' unnastand . . ."

"Put him on," said Montalbano, turning on the speakerphone.

"Help . . . help . . . for heaven's sake, please help me . . ." It was the voice of an elderly or ill man, a feeble, desperate voice. Fazio leapt out of his chair.

"Try to stay calm. And please tell me your name and where you live," said the inspector.

"Wait just a minute . . . no, no, I can't do it, I can't remember what my name is . . ."

"Try to make an effort, please. What is your name?"

"I'm confused . . . wait . . . it's coming to me . . . ah, yes, that's it . . . my name is Jacono . . . help . . ."

"Try to remain as calm as possible and tell me where you live."

"I live in the country . . ."

"Yes, but where, exactly?"

"I think the district is called Zicari . . . no . . . no . . . wait . . . Ficarra . . . Ficarra district . . . come quickly . . . hurry . . . help . . ."

Fazio repeated to himself, "Jacono, Ficarra district," as if to commit it to memory, and dashed out of the room.

"Mr Jacono, can you hear me?"

"I don't understand . . . don't understand . . ."

"What don't you understand?"

"My daughter . . . my daughter hasn't come . . ."

"Did you have an appointment with your daughter?"

"No . . . no appointment . . ."

Fazio came back in.

"Gallo's ready. He's worked out where the man lives."

"How long will it take to get there?"

"With Gallo, about fifteen minutes."

"Mr Jacono, don't worry, don't get upset, just stay where you are and don't do anything. We'll be at your house shortly."

"Come quick . . . quick . . ."

They ran out of the station, got into the car, and Gallo took off like a rocket, putting the siren on.

Turning off the main road to Montereale, they took the first country road on the right and then turned left at the crossroads. And very nearly crashed straight into an empty car poorly parked on the verge.

Fazio hurled a few curses at whoever had left it there.

"We're already in the Ficarra district here," said Gallo.

"Stop in front of the second house," said Fazio.

The second house was right on the road. The garden was at the back.

It was a two-storey house and looked well maintained. The front door was closed, while an upstairs window was open.

They got out of the car.

"Be quiet and keep your ears peeled," said Montalbano.

Then he shouted as loudly as he could: "Mr Jacono! We're here!"

In the deep silence that followed, all three of them distinctly heard a far-away voice.

"Help! Help!"

It was coming from the open window.

"Let's break down the front door," said Fazio.

"Wait a second," said Gallo, studying the front of the house carefully. "I think I can climb up to that window."

And before the inspector could stop him, he was standing on top of the iron grate over a ground-floor window beside the door, which he'd used as a ladder; then, holding on to a drainpipe, he set one foot on the arch over the door, put all his weight on it, and sprang forward, seizing hold of the windowsill with both hands.

"The cock's turned into a monkey! Well done!" Montalbano said in admiration.

With one last effort Gallo hoisted himself up and sat down on the windowsill. He glanced inside the room and said:

"There's a man lying on the floor groaning. I don't see any blood. There's also a wheelchair here. I think he's paralytic and must have fallen. Let me give him a hand and then I'll come down and let you in."

It took Jacono more than half an hour to calm down a little and tell them what had happened to him.

Fazio had found a box of camomile tea in the kitchen and made him a double dose.

Jacono, whose first name was Carlo, was seventy-seven years old and had been a business executive. He enjoyed a comfortable retirement, sharing a home with his daughter Luigia, aged thirty-eight, who was a clerk at the Banca Cooperativa di Vigàta and finished work at half-past four. He had another daughter, Gisella, who lived with her husband in Montereale. During the day a cleaner by the name of Grazia looked after him.

But that afternoon something strange had happened that had never happened before. Luigia had called his mobile at four thirty-five and told him he could send Grazia home, because she was on her way there.

Jacono, not feeling well, had lain down in bed with his clothes on, trusting his daughter to be punctual, since she was never so much as a minute late for anything, said goodbye to the cleaner, and remained there alone.

But at half-past five, seeing that Luigia hadn't come home yet, he tried calling her on her mobile. Which was turned off. He tried again two or three more times, always with the same result.

And so he tried calling Gisella, his other daughter, but her line was busy.

Feeling restless and afraid, he tried to get up and sit in the wheelchair but fell to the floor.

Luckily he hadn't lost his grip of the phone, and that was how he'd been able to call the police.

"Was your daughter on her way here in her car?"

"Of course."

"What kind of car is it?"

"A Volkswagen Polo. Licence number BU 329 KJ."

Gallo and the inspector exchanged glances, and they understood each other at once. The awkwardly parked car they'd almost hit at the crossroads was a Polo.

CHAPTER
SIX

"*Papà! Papà!*" a woman called from the road.

Gisella had arrived, having been alerted by Fazio.

Montalbano got up, left the room almost running, and stopped the woman before she started climbing the stairs to go to her father's bedroom.

"I'm Inspector Montalbano."

"What are you doing here?"

"Your father called us here. He'd fallen and wasn't able to —"

"Oh, my God! What's happening? On my way here I saw my sister's car stopped at the crossroads. Where is she? And how is Papa?"

"Listen to me for a moment. Your father is very upset but is all right. Just don't tell him about your sister's car."

"Why?"

"Because he would just get more upset. And he's practically in a state of confusion. Do you have a recent photo of Luigia?"

"A photo?! What on earth is going on? Where is Luigia?"

"At the moment I'm unable to tell you anything. But, please, the photo."

"There are some in her room."

"Then please go upstairs and get one before going into your father's room, and you can give it to me when you see me out."

They went upstairs. Montalbano went into Jacono's room, and Gisella continued on down the hallway.

"Your daughter Gisella is here. She's just gone to the bathroom for a moment. We're going to go now, Mr Jacono, since we know you'll be in good hands."

"And what about Luigia? . . . Where's Luigia? Why is she so late?" Jacono wailed.

"Mr Jacono, please don't worry. We'll let you know as soon as we have any news of your daughter."

Gisella, meanwhile, had arrived, and ran at once into her father's arms to comfort him.

"We'll be seeing you, signora," the inspector said to her.

"Let me show you out," said Gisella.

Montalbano didn't even have time to settle down comfortably and buckle his seat belt before Gallo was screeching to a halt, nose to nose with the Polo.

It was starting to get dark.

Montalbano jumped out and grabbed the handle to the driver's-side door of the Polo, which immediately opened. The key was in the ignition, with other keys hanging from the ring. On the passenger's seat was a rather elegant handbag.

The inspector picked it up, opened it, and looked inside. The woman's mobile phone was there, turned off, along with a purse with two hundred euros, some lipstick, a handkerchief, and another set of keys.

"Boys," he said, "I am convinced we are looking at a third kidnapping."

"What can we do?" Fazio asked anxiously.

Montalbano handed him the handbag. Then he took the key out of the ignition, locked the car doors with another key, and gave them all to Fazio.

"Let's hurry back to Vigàta. Once we're across town, Fazio, you go into the station and inform the commissioner's office. Gallo and I will continue to Montelusa."

"What are you going to do?"

"We can't keep these kidnappings secret any longer. I'm going to spill all the beans on TV."

Nicolò Zito, editor in chief of the Free Channel's news department, was a friend of the inspector's and made himself immediately available.

It took them only fifteen minutes to record an interview. Then they played it back and watched.

Zito appeared first, saying:

"*We will now broadcast an important request by Chief Inspector of Vigàta Police Salvo Montalbano.*"

The inspector appeared on-screen.

"*We have reason to believe that this woman whose face you see in this photograph*" — and here Montalbano's face disappeared and in its place appeared the photo Gisella had given him, as the inspector continued speaking in the background — "*was the victim of a kidnapping that took place this afternoon between four-thirty and five o'clock, along* the country road that leads from the Vigàta — Montereale provincial road to the district of Ficarra."

Montalbano's face returned.

"Anyone who may have seen anything unusual at the time and place mentioned, we ask you please to inform the Vigàta Police. The woman in question was driving a Volkswagen Polo, which was found at the spot where she was abducted. Thank you."

The camera then pulled back until Zito was visible beside the inspector.

"Inspector Montalbano, do you think we are looking at a kidnapping for ransom?"

"Unfortunately no, which makes the whole case more difficult. We are dealing with a maniac here, one who abducts his victims and —"

"Are you saying there have been other such cases?"

"Yes. Two others."

"Did the abductor harm the victims?"

"So far he hasn't hurt any of his victims. He limits himself to rendering them unconscious with chloroform, but doesn't steal anything and doesn't even touch their clothes. But we can't rule out that he might change his methods."

"Thank you, Inspector Montalbano."

"Thank you, sir."

"I'll broadcast it on the ten o'clock news and then run it again on the midnight edition."

"Fazio in?"

"Nah, Chief, 'e's atta scene o' the kidnappin' insomuch as the guys o' the Flyin' Squat wannit 'im

72

onna scene an' axed 'im to come cuz 'e knew more stuff 'n 'em, 'em meanin' the Flyin' Squat. But Isspecter Augello's 'ere onna premisses."

Montalbano knocked on the door to Mimi's office, went in, and sat down.

"Both girls recognized their belongings. So we can conclude the car was used for the abductions," said Mimi.

"Apparently he's changed cars," the inspector said bitterly.

"Yeah, I'd heard the latest good news. So I got to work."

"Meaning what?"

"I am now in a position to tell you that there have been no reports of stolen cars."

"That doesn't mean the abductor is using his own. He may just have taken another whose owner hasn't noticed yet."

"Were you expecting this third abduction?"

"Yes, Mimi, which is why I just can't find any peace."

"But what fault is it of yours?"

"Oh, it's my fault, all right — completely!"

"In what sense?"

"You see, Mimi, the first two abductions were carried out in exactly the same way. A car stopped by the side of the road with its bonnet up and a man bent over seeming to be working on the engine. At that point I should have issued a warning to all women driving alone not to stop if they saw such a scene. If I had given that simple warning, this third kidnapping would never have happened."

"Well, in my opinion, it's actually good you didn't do it."

"Why?"

"Because you would have sowed panic, and who knows? Maybe some poor bloke whose car broke down would've been lynched by a mob."

The inspector told him about the appeal he'd made on television. Augello glanced at his watch. It was past nine.

"I'll make you an offer," he said. "Since someone's going to have to wait around for phone calls, and so there's a chance we're going to have to spend the night here, what do you say if I go home now, and you stay here, and at three o'clock tomorrow morning, I'll come in and relieve you?"

"Offer accepted," said Montalbano, getting up and going out.

From his office he rang Catarella.

"Come into my office for a second, Cat, would you?"

Catarella came running.

"At your service, sir!"

"Cat, I'm going to have to stay here tonight till three. I'll be waiting for some important phone calls. What time do you get off?"

"At ten, Chief."

"And who takes over for you?"

"Intelisano, Chief."

"When Intelisano comes in, tell him to come into my office before he goes on the job."

"Chief, beckin' yer partin' an' all, but I'm not gonna tell Intelisano nuttin'."

74

Montalbano couldn't believe his ears. Was the end of the world nigh? Catarella refusing to carry out an order?

"Cat, what's got into you?"

"Wha'ss gat inna me izzat if yer gonna be here till tree a'clack, I'm gonna stay 'ere till tree a'clack, too, an' even till four, an' if you —"

"OK, OK." The inspector cut him off. "But I want you to be careful with those phone calls. Don't ask any questions and pass them straight to my office. Oh, and, while you're at it, send someone down to buy four panini and two beers. What kind of panini do you want?"

"Wit' salami, Chief."

"Me, too. Here, let me give you the money."

"Oh, Jesus, what fun!" Catarella cried out, practically with tears in his eyes.

"What's so fun?"

"Eatin' panini an' salami wit' yiz, Chief!"

Fazio came in as Catarella was going out.

"Any news?" Montalbano asked.

Fazio gestured dejectedly.

"Forensics took the car to Montelusa to see if they could find any fingerprints; the Flying Squad is combing the area, but I don't think they'll find anything."

It was ten o'clock.

"Come with me," Montalbano said to him.

They went into Augello's office, which had a television, and turned it on. Zito had placed the inspector's public appeal at the front of the newscast, right after the logo and credits.

They watched it and then turned off the set.

"I'm available if you want to man the phone in shifts," Fazio offered.

"Already taken care of," said Montalbano.

It gave him immense satisfaction to utter the very same phrase Fazio used all too often, which normally got terribly on his nerves. He continued:

"You can go home now and come back in at eight tomorrow morning. That way Mimì can go home and get a little sleep."

The first phone call, which came in at ten-forty, was not the one he'd been expecting, and it made him choke on his panino.

"Ahh, Chief, Chief! Ahh, Chief!"

This lament was normally Catarella's refrain whenever "Hizzoner the C'mishner" called.

"Is it the commissioner?"

"Yeah, Chief, iss 'im poissonally in poisson! An' 'is voice sounds like a lion roarin'!"

"Well, let's let him roar! Put him on."

"Montalbano!"

"What can I do for you, sir?"

"Montalbano!"

Had His Honour the Commissioner gone deaf or something?

"I'm right here!" said the inspector, raising his voice.

"I've just found out — purely by chance, mind you — from a local television station that it took you three abductions before you deigned to inform the proper authorities, which means that you kept the first two hidden. Is that correct?"

He had no choice but to say yes. He hadn't alerted "the proper authorities" because he'd completely forgotten to do so.

"Yes, Mr Commissioner, but, you see —"

"No buts!"

"Is it all right if I say 'if' instead of 'but'?"

"Don't try to make light of this! It's really not the right time!"

"I would never presume to —"

"I'll be waiting for you tomorrow morning, at nine o'clock sharp!"

And he hung up.

Montalbano took a sip of beer and called Livia to inform her of the situation.

When they'd finished talking, he came to the conclusion that, between one panino and the next, a cigarette would fit in quite nicely. Should he go outside to smoke it, or break the rules and smoke it in his office?

He decided on the middle way. He got up, went over to the window, opened it, and smoked his cigarette with his elbows propped up on the windowsill.

The telephone rang. He ran over and picked up the receiver.

"Am I speaking to Inspector Montalbano?"

It was the cold-congested voice of a middle-aged man.

"Yes, that's me."

"I wanted to tell you that that woman, who is a terrible sinner and a common slut, will suffer the punishment she deserves amidst the flames of hell. Her fate is irrevocably sealed by now. You will never see her again."

"Mind telling me who this is speaking?"

"You, too, wretched sinner, will meet the same end."

"But who is speaking?"

"The King of the Light."

"Then please get me the King of the Gas, because they overcharged me on the last bill."

And he slammed the receiver down.

He had better get used to it, however, because he was sure to receive more crank calls as the night wore on. An appeal like the one he'd made on TV was like honey to flies — an irresistible invitation for the unhinged, the pathological liars, and those with too much time on their hands. Half an hour later — after he'd spent the time on a crossword puzzle — the telephone rang.

"My name is Armando Riccobono, and I would like to speak to Inspector —"

"I'm Inspector Montalbano."

"This is about that kidnapping you talked about on the Free Channel."

"Did you see something?"

"I think so."

"Tell me about it."

"I have a house in Ficarra. This afternoon I got in my car to drive to Vigàta. It was probably around a quarter to five or a little later. When I got to the crossroads that lead to the provincial road, I saw, on the other side of the same road, just past the crossroads, a car stopped with its bonnet raised. When I turned left I saw Signora Luigia in her car, coming up. And that's what I had to say."

The timing corresponded.

"Were you able to see whether there was also a man near the stopped car?"

"I didn't see anyone. If there was a man bending down under the raised bonnet, I wouldn't have been able to see him from where I was."

"Thank you, Mr Riccobono. Could you please leave me your telephone number?"

Montalbano wrote the number down on a piece of paper, thanked the man, and hung up.

Riccobono's testimony meant that the third abduction was carried out using exactly the same strategy as the other two. Could one still consider the fact that the third woman also worked in a bank a coincidence?

The telephone rang again. It was Fazio.

"Chief, did you watch Tele Vigàta?"

That was the other local television station.

"No, why?"

"Because they aired an emergency news broadcast in which they gave the names of the three women who'd been abducted and also mentioned that all three worked in banks."

Montalbano launched into a litany of curses. "How the hell did they find out?"

"They said they'd received an anonymous phone call."

"Logically speaking, the only person who could have made that call was the abductor himself."

"Yeah, I was thinking the same thing. But for what purpose?"

"To put us on the wrong track."

"And what track would that be?"

"To have us and the whole town believe that this is some form of action against the banks."

"So why do you think that's not the right track?"

"First, because the thought's being put in our heads by the abductor himself. Second, for the reason we've already said: how are these overnight kidnappings doing any harm to the banks? They're not. On top of everything else, the first two women abducted didn't even miss a single hour of work."

When he'd finished talking to Fazio, he picked up the crossword puzzle again but didn't have time to read a clue before the telephone called him back to duty.

"This is the CABC calling!" said an imperious voice.

What the hell was the CABC?

"I'm sorry, what was that?"

"The CABC!"

"And what does that stand for?"

"It stands for Clandestine Anti-Bank Coalition. Do you want to know what our goal is?"

"Why not?" the inspector asked benevolently.

"Our goal is to terrorize everyone who works at banks, so they will resign and the banks will be forced to close for lack of personnel. You should know that the CABC is a worldwide, international organization which —"

The inspector hung up and went back to his crossword.

Nothing else happened. Dead calm.

Mimì Augello showed up at five past three. He was still half asleep and constantly yawning.

"Get any interesting phone calls?" he asked.

"No, except for one from a certain Riccobono."

He'd just finished telling him about it when the phone rang again.

"Shall I answer, or should you?" asked Mimì.

"You get it. But if you don't mind, turn on the speakerphone."

"My name is Roscitano . . . I would like to speak immediately with the head of the police station, what's his name . . . Montalbano."

The man sounded rather agitated.

"You can tell me. I'm Inspector Augello."

"Well, when I went down into the garage to get my car I saw, on the ground, in front of the rolling shutter, a woman completely naked and covered in blood and moaning in pain."

"Did she say what her name was?"

"She won't speak! She just groans. I think she's in shock. My wife brought her into our house."

"Tell us where you live."

"Just a kilometre past the Scala dei Turchi, on the provincial road to Montereale."

"Can you be more specific?"

"It's hard to miss. It's a little red house with a turret, right by the sea."

"We'll be right over."

"Listen, is it OK if I leave in the meantime?"

"Why? Where do you have to go?"

"To Palermo, to pick up my son, who's arriving on the mail boat from Naples."

"I'm sorry, but you can't."

"Are you kidding me? But my son —"

"If you're not there when I get to your house, I will have you arrested the moment you enter Palermo."

The man cursed, and Mimì hung up.

"Come on," said Montalbano. "Let's get moving."

"We can take my car," said Augello.

"Come on inside. It's right this way," said the fat, fiftyish Mrs Agata Roscitano, leading them towards the bedroom. "I washed the poor girl and disinfected her wounds. There must be at least thirty of them . . ."

Montalbano stopped in his tracks. "What do you mean, thirty?"

"Oh, I mean thirty, maybe even more. Made with the tip of a knife but not very deep. I'm a trained nurse, and I know what I'm talking about. Only the girl's face was spared. She's resting now, so please be quiet."

They tiptoed into the room and approached the bed. The inspector recognized her at once.

It was Luigia Jacono.

CHAPTER
SEVEN

The young woman kept moaning softly, thrashing about in her sleep.

"Let's let her rest," said Montalbano, making for the door.

As soon as they were in the dining room, the inspector told Augello to alert the Flying Squad that the missing woman had been found and that they should send a doctor to examine her.

Then he turned to Roscitano.

"Did you hear any cars in the area last night?"

"I didn't hear anything."

"I know exactly what the inspector is asking," Signora Agata intervened.

"And what's that?"

"You want to know whether the girl was brought here in a car and then abandoned, or came here by herself."

"That's right. And did you hear anything?"

"No, nothing. But I can tell you anyway that she came here by herself, after walking a great distance."

"How do you know that?"

"From the condition of her feet, which are a shambles. She must have walked barefoot across the countryside. Her poor feet are like big open wounds."

Augello returned from making his phone calls.

"The Flying Squad will be here shortly with a doctor."

"Mimì, I want you to make another call for me. To Jacono's house. The number's here, on this little piece of paper. It's possible the one who answers will be Gisella, Luigia's sister."

"And what should I tell her?"

"Tell her that Luigia's all right, and that for the moment she's not coming home because we still have to question her."

Augello stepped out again to make the call.

"Shall I make you some coffee?" asked Signora Agata. Montalbano accepted the offer with enthusiasm.

As the signora went into the kitchen, the inspector turned to Roscitano.

"When you first saw the young woman on the ground in front of the shutter," he said, "what did you do? Did you go up to her?"

"Of course."

"Did you touch her?"

"Why should I have touched her?"

"To see if she was still alive."

"I didn't need to touch her to know that! She was groaning. Faintly, but groaning just the same."

"Is that all?"

"What do you mean?"

"Did she say anything?"

"She said something when my wife and I picked her up to carry her into the house. She said, 'call'."

"No, she didn't say 'call', she said 'car'," said Signora Agata, coming in with the coffee.

"She said, 'call'!" Roscitano fired back in irritation.

"No, sir, she clearly said 'car'."

Mimì came back into the room and took a cup of coffee.

"I spoke to the sister and put her mind at rest," he said.

After the coffee, Montalbano naturally felt like smoking a cigarette. He went out of the house, with Augello following behind.

It was a soft night, clear and windless. The sea lay sleeping a short distance away. They could tell from the gentle, rhythmic sound of the surf.

"You seem worried."

"I am worried. The kidnapper has raised his line of fire, as I'd been expecting. Thirty knife wounds, however superficial, are no joke. What will he do next time?"

"Do you think he may also have raped her?"

"Anything's possible with a madman like that, but I don't think so."

"Tell me why."

"Because I'm more than convinced that these abductions are not being carried out for sexual purposes."

In the distance, amid the silence of the night, they began to hear the wail of the police sirens as their colleagues drew near.

"Some people really enjoy waking up people trying to sleep!" Montalbano commented on his way back into the house.

★ ★ ★

The travelling circus, consisting of the chief of the Flying Squad, the public prosecutor, Tommaseo, and a doctor, Amelia Sinatra, arrived in a convoy of four cars and an ambulance and came to a noisy halt right outside the door.

Dr Sinatra went immediately into the house.

Galeassi, chief of the Flying Squad, got out of his car and said to Montalbano:

"We're going to see how she's feeling and whether or not it's a good time to question her. At any rate, the investigation's in my hands. Got that?"

"Got it."

As a result, the inspector and Mimì Augello stayed outside. But it was all for naught.

Indeed, an hour and a half later, Galeassi came out and said angrily to Montalbano, as though it was somehow his fault: "But that woman can't recall a damn thing!"

Then Prosecutor Tommaseo emerged. "It seems she wasn't raped."

He was clearly disappointed, since he lived for crimes of passion, rapes, and other forms of sexual violence against women.

Exiting after him were Dr Sinatra followed by two ambulance attendants carrying Luigia on a stretcher. They loaded her into the ambulance and drove off.

Montalbano and Augello said goodbye to the Roscitanos, thanked them for everything, excused themselves for the disturbance, got into their car, and headed for Vigàta.

86

Once they were on the road, Mimì asked a precise question.

"To judge from appearances, you were right about the whole thing turning more violent. But tell me in all honesty: what is going through your mind?"

"Mimì, among the many things Manuela Smerca told us there was one in particular that I think was absolutely correct."

"And what was that?"

"That this man is frightened by his own actions. And what he did to Luigia confirms this."

"Help me understand."

"He probably would have liked to murder the girl this time around, but he didn't have the nerve to do it, so he limited himself to torturing her with thirty superficial knife cuts."

"But that could be the work of a sadist."

"It could be, but it isn't. I would bet that he inflicted the knife wounds on Luigia when she was passed out from the chloroform. A sadist wants his victim to be squirming and pleading and wailing in pain, for his enjoyment."

"All right, but where does this lead us?"

"To the most dangerous category of all, Mimì."

"And what would that be?"

"That category of people who by nature are not given to harming others, but who, once they've done it, are capable of doing anything to cover up what they've done."

"Because they're afraid to fall in people's estimation of them?"

"That, too, but above all because they themselves would never get over the shame they would feel if the act were discovered."

"So what I think you're saying is that you're of the opinion that the person doing these things is a man above suspicion?"

"Yes, Mimì, that's exactly right." He heaved a big sigh.

"This is one of those typical cases you can break your head over," he continued. "And I just wish . . ."

He trailed off.

"You just wish what?"

"I just wish I was twenty years younger, Mimì."

What can a man do who comes home at seven in the morning after a sleepless night and has an appointment with his superior at nine in Montelusa?

He can do nothing but what the inspector did. Take all his clothes off, get into the shower, shave, put on some clean underwear, put the coffeepot on the stove, don a clean suit from the wardrobe, drink an entire mug of black coffee, get into the car, and drive to Montelusa.

Since he knew the reason for the commissioner's summons, he prepared a response that was a tremendous lie as big as a skyscraper.

Going into the commissioner's waiting room, he looked at his watch. Five to nine.

"I have an appointment with His Honour the Commissioner," he said to a uniformed officer sitting behind a desk.

The cop looked at a piece of paper in front of him. "Yes, I know, Inspector Montalbano, but the commissioner is busy at the moment. If you'd like to take a seat . . ."

Montalbano sat down on a small sofa exactly like the one in his dentist's office.

Suddenly, and for no apparent reason, this thought made the last tooth on the left upper row of his mouth start hurting a little.

He touched it carefully with the tip of his tongue. It did hurt, there was no getting around it. This brought on a sudden attack of the nerves, and he began squirming on the sofa.

Nothing in the world scared him so much as having to sit in a dentist's chair. Only those sentenced to death, perhaps, when being placed in the electric chair, experienced a comparable terror.

And when was Hizzoner the C'mishner going to be free, anyway?

Great. Now the inspector felt himself getting all sweaty.

He began to feel an overwhelming desire to get up and go. So he stood up, and at that exact moment the telephone on the officer's table rang. Montalbano didn't move. The officer listened, then said:

"You can go in now."

The inspector knocked gently, opened the door, and went in.

"Good morning," he said.

The commissioner didn't return his greeting, but merely put down a sheet of paper he'd been reading, looked at Montalbano, who was standing stiff as a pole before him, drummed his fingers on the desk, and finally said:

"Montalbano, I will get immediately to the point, because I find your presence irksome."

"Then please get to the point, Mr Commissioner."

"Would you mind telling me for what mysterious reason you decided not to inform any of your superiors about the abductions that were occurring and unfortunately are still occurring in Vigàta?"

"If I —"

"Actually, before you say anything, I want to warn you that your answer to my question will determine whether or not I decide to take measures against you. Do you understand me?"

"Sure."

"Now go ahead and speak."

For a fraction of a second, Montalbano closed his eyes, then took the plunge.

"I was following orders, Mr Commissioner."

Bonetti-Alderighi looked at him in shock. "Following orders?!"

"That's right, sir. And you have no idea how many sleepless nights it has cost me, since I was forced to ignore my most basic duties in obeying such an order from above."

"From above? But from whom?"

"From His Excellency the Undersecretary Macannuco, who is the uncle, on the mother's side, of the first girl who was abducted. He called me straightaway and ordered me to remain absolutely silent about the whole thing, with everyone. He didn't want his niece . . . Do you know Macannuco?"

"Not personally."

"If you did, you would understand. He's a very vindictive man. If I'd refused, he would never have let me forget it."

The commissioner's attitude changed immediately. He certainly didn't want to jeopardize his own career.

"Please sit down."

The inspector sat down.

"Have you known Macannuco for a long time?"

"Since elementary school."

"But then why didn't you tell me about the second abduction?"

"Because when you finally did find out that there had been a first abduction, you would have got angry with me and —"

"All right, then, let's not talk about it any further," he said, interrupting him.

They chatted amicably for another five minutes or so, after which the commissioner dismissed Montalbano, absolving him of all his sins, except for original sin, which did not fall under his jurisdiction.

Once out of the building, Montalbano no longer had a toothache.

In speaking with the commissioner, he'd learned that Luigia had been taken to San Giacomo Hospital, and so, since he was already in Montelusa, he might as well go and check in on her and possibly talk to her about the abduction.

The nun, or whatever she was, sitting behind a reception desk that was all telephones, computers, and devices with red and green lights incessantly flashing as on a Christmas tree, carefully read the inspector's police ID card, studied him long and hard to determine whether he really looked like the photo, then said, as she handed him back his card: "Room 29, second floor."

And this was where the trouble began.

Because not once in the inspector's life had he entered a hospital without getting lost.

Having found the lift with some effort, since it was strategically hidden by a giant fuchsia plant on one side and a statue of San Giacomo on the other, the inspector pushed the button to summon it to the ground floor.

After a short wait, the lift arrived, empty. He went in and pushed button number 2. The lift took off and, barely thirty seconds later, stopped.

Montalbano got out, took a few steps, but then realized he was walking down a darkened, dusty corridor full of half-open cardboard boxes, bottomless chairs, and broken bed frames. Instead of going upstairs the lift had gone down and taken him into a basement.

Turning around to get back into the lift, he could no longer find it. It had disappeared. How was that possible? He took three steps forward, three steps back, all the while feeling the wall. He turned around to the opposite wall, felt its surface as well. Nothing. The wall was solid.

92

There was no trace of a lift.

He began to get scared.

The basement was utterly deserted. If he didn't quickly find a way to get back upstairs, he was sure to remain stuck down there for days. And he would likely die of hunger and thirst, a horrible end, the thought of which made his hair stand straight up like fresh spinach.

As a sense of panic came over him, his head started to spin, and he leaned his back against the wall. At which point the wall behind him opened up, and he lost his balance, staggered two steps backwards, arms rotating in the air like the blades of a windmill, and suddenly found himself back inside the lift.

This time it took him to the second floor.

As soon as he was in the hallway, however, he froze.

What was that room number? With the fright he'd just had, he'd forgotten.

So how was he going to get out of this now?

There was no question whatsoever of getting back in that accursed lift and returning to the reception desk. No way, not even at knifepoint.

Luckily, he spotted a nurse coming towards him. He told her the young woman's name and she told him her room number. He knocked on the door to room 29, but there was no answer. So he turned the doorknob and went in.

Luigia was lying with her eyes closed and breathing calmly and evenly.

Montalbano sat down in a chair right beside the bed. The young woman must have sensed his presence there, because moments later she opened her eyes, blinked a few times, brought her vision into focus, and looked at him questioningly.

"I am Inspector Montalbano, of the Vigàta Police. I'm in charge of the case. How do you feel?"

"I'm recovering."

"Would it bother you to talk about what happened?"

"Well, yes, it would, and it makes me feel very anxious, but I don't think it can be avoided."

"Have you been in touch with your family?"

"This morning my sister came to visit."

"Want to tell me how the whole thing unfolded?"

The woman told him. At first the abduction was a carbon copy of the previous ones. A car stopped at the side of the road with the bonnet up, a man asking for help, she pulling over, he pointing a handgun at her, forcing her out of the car, and knocking her out with chloroform.

Then came the second part, and here there were some new twists.

Waking up a few hours later, naked and hurting all over, terrified to find herself covered in blood, and not knowing what had happened to her, she started looking around for help, but found none.

She walked for a while — but couldn't say for how long — losing blood until she finally collapsed, exhausted and disoriented, outside a metal shutter, no longer able to move.

"Were you able to see your abductor's face?"

"Well, only in a manner of speaking. I couldn't really describe his face, because he was wearing a cap pulled

94

down practically over his eyes, dark sunglasses, and a large scarf that covered the lower part of his face."

"What kind of voice did he have? Was it gravelly, nasal . . .?"

"He never spoke."

"Then how was he able to tell you to get out of the car?"

"By gesturing with the hand that was holding the gun."

"In which hand was he holding the gun?"

"In his right hand. I don't think he was left-handed."

"And were you unconscious when he inflicted those wounds on you?"

"Yes, but they're not actually wounds; they're more like scratches of varying depth."

"In your opinion, was your abductor a young man or an older man?"

Luigia answered at once: "An older man."

"Did your sister tell you that it was a couple living near the Scala dei Turchi who finally rescued you?"

"Yes, she did."

"Now please listen to me carefully. Apparently, when that couple was picking you up off the ground to take you to their house, you said a word with a clear meaning."

"I had the strength to speak?" the young woman asked, sincerely surprised.

"Not to speak, but to say one word."

"What word was that?"

"Well, that's the question. The man insists that you said 'call', while his wife is sure that you said 'car'."

Luigia, looking intently at the inspector, rolled her eyes upon hearing the word "car".

"What difference does it make?" she asked after a pause.

"It makes a tremendous difference. If you said 'car' when only half-conscious, this might mean you recognized the car stopped at the side of the road, the kidnapper's car. Which I'm sure he stole."

"No, the car I saw wasn't anything I recognized," Luigia said firmly.

"Do you know much about cars?"

"Nothing at all."

"Could you perhaps describe it to me anyway, tell me what colour it was . . .?"

"I really didn't pay any attention to that, believe me . . ."

At this point Montalbano asked her a question without knowing why he was asking it.

"Has anyone told you you are the third?"

"The third what?"

"The third woman abducted in an overnight kidnapping."

"So there were two other kidnappings before me?"

Her tone was that of someone unable to accept what she has just heard.

"Yes, except that the other two girls were released with all their clothes on and hadn't been harmed or suffered violence in any way. But there is a strange coincidence which may not mean anything: the other two girls also worked at banks."

Luigia closed her eyes.

"I'm sorry, but I suddenly feel very tired."

"Then I'll leave you in peace," said Montalbano, standing up. "But if in the meantime any details about the abductor's stolen car come back to you —"

"How can you be so sure that it was a stolen car?"

"Because in the first two cases, the kidnapper used a car he'd stolen, which he then set fire to. Anyway, to repeat: if you happen to remember anything, please call me at police headquarters."

And he went out, thinking that Mrs Roscitano was probably right, that Luigia had said "car" and not "call".

CHAPTER
EIGHT

"Ahh, Chief! A' nine a'clack this mornin' Mr Pitruzzo came an' said 'e 'ad a 'pointmint wit' yiz . . ."

Montalbano slapped himself on the forehead. Virduzzo! Damn his porous memory! He'd forgotten completely about that appointment!

"Did he leave a message?"

"Nuttin', Chief. After spennin' an hour waitin' inna waitin' room, he come an' says he cou'n't wait no more . . ."

"Oh, well. He'll be back. Send Fazio and Inspector Augello to my office, would you?"

The first to arrive was Fazio, who'd already been told by Augello that they'd found Luigia.

"Any news of Di Carlo?" Montalbano asked him.

"None whatsoever. I'm gathering information on him from a variety of people. As soon as I have a clear picture, I'll let you know."

"Here I am," said Augello, coming in. "And a good morning to all, even though I haven't slept a wink."

"Have a seat and let's talk a little," said the inspector. "Just now, Fazio told me there's no news of Di Carlo. And since the girl he's in love with has not come forward to report his disappearance to me, this means either that she knows where he is or that she is in no condition to move about freely. Are you two in agreement?"

"We agree," said Fazio and Augello.

"Therefore we absolutely need to find out who this girl is; we have to be able to give her a first and last name."

"It won't be easy," said Fazio.

"But we do have a precise starting point," said the inspector. "We know for certain where the girl spent her holiday. She was in Tenerife in July and in Lanzarote in August. How many travel agencies are there in Vigàta?"

"Four," replied Fazio.

"I'd try my luck with them."

"I'll drop in on them this afternoon."

"I have the feeling we're not going to find out anything from these agencies," Augello cut in.

"Why?"

"Because, Salvo, you're a little too o — I mean, you're behind the times, dear Salvo. Nowadays everybody does everything through the internet."

It was clear he was about to say he was too old but managed to correct himself in time. Montalbano absorbed the blow but didn't let anything show.

"Well, Fazio's going to give it a try just the same. Now, to the overnight kidnappings. This morning I went to the hospital to talk to Luigia Jacono. Mimì, do you remember what Roscitano said to us about when they were carrying Luigia half-conscious into their house, when he said Luigia had said 'call', but his wife said the word she'd said was 'car'?"

"Yes, I remember perfectly."

"When I told Luigia about it, she said she couldn't remember a thing about the car. But I was under the impression she wasn't being sincere."

"What reason would she have for that?" asked Augello.

"I don't know. And there's more. When she learned from me that hers was the third recent case of abduction, she had a strange reaction. She was surprised, as if she'd expected to be the only one."

"What does that mean?" asked Augello.

"I'll try to explain. In my opinion, Luigia was convinced that the kidnapping, as well as the thirty superficial knife wounds, was something that concerned her and only her."

"Are you trying to tell me that she was more or less expecting what happened to her?" Augello pressed him.

"That's exactly what I'm trying to tell you. And this means that the girl's hiding something."

"Wait a second," said Augello. "In plain language, you're saying that Luigia must have done something to someone that made her expect or fear some sort of revenge?"

"I could be wrong, but I think that if that's not the way it is, then the truth isn't too far off. But Luigia won't talk, of that I am sure. Therefore it's up to you, Mimì, to get close to her."

"With pleasure," Augello consented.

"But don't take your time about it. The sooner we can stop this kidnapper, the better. After what he did to

Luigia Jacono, I'm starting to get seriously worried. Now that he's tasted blood, the next victim he deposits in the countryside for us might well be dead."

A heavy silence descended on them, then was shattered by the telephone.

"Ahh, Chief, 'ere'd be a soitain Mr Lo Curto onna line 'at oigently wants a talk t'yiz poissonally in poisson . . ."

"OK."

"Inspector Montalbano?"

"What can I do for you, Mr Lo Curto?"

"Lo Curzio's the name. Alessandro Lo Curzio."

Montalbano cursed the saints in his mind and sent another powerful curse in Catarella's direction.

"I'm sorry, please go ahead."

"I'm manager of the Vigàta branch of the Banca di Trinacria, and I need to meet you as soon as possible."

"Is it something urgent?"

"Extremely urgent."

The inspector glanced at his watch. He had an hour at his disposal.

"If you like you can come here right now."

"Thank you. I'll be there in about fifteen minutes."

Montalbano adjourned the meeting.

"OK, boys, time to get down to work. We'll meet again as soon as we have something to report."

Alessandro Lo Curzio looked to be in his early forties. Tall, elegant, in good physical condition, cologne-scented, tanned, and with a smile that one needed sunglasses to look at.

It was clear he was destined for the sort of brilliant career common to so many of today's executives: a rapid ascent (perhaps from selling his own mother to the highest bidder), arrival at the top, immediate crash of the stock value of the company, bank, or whatever it was, disappearance of said executive, and reappearance, one year later, of same executive in a position of even greater importance.

"I'm also here on behalf of my colleague Federico Molisano, manager of the local branch of Credito Marittimo."

"What have you got to tell me?"

"That both Molisano and I have a problem. A big problem that risks becoming a nuisance."

"Please explain."

"There are three women working at my branch; there's just one at Molisano's. They've probably all spoken to each other and are operating together; whatever the case, their intention is to stop working in banks."

Montalbano understood.

"Are they afraid of being abducted?"

"Well, yes. They said to themselves: so far we've seen a woman from the Banco Siculo, another from the Banca di Credito, and another from the Banca Cooperativa abducted, and soon we'll be next."

Oh, there were a lot of banks in Vigàta! The most amazing thing was that the more the town sank into poverty and misery — with factories shut down, shops declaring bankruptcy, unemployment rates through the roof — the more banks sprang up. How did one explain such a mystery?

"So what is it, exactly, you would like me to do?"

"Provide the four women with an armed escort."

"I'm terribly sorry, but I think you've got the wrong address."

"Why?"

"Because I'm a mere inspector. That's not the sort of thing I can decide for myself. It's beyond my jurisdiction."

"So who should I turn to, then?"

"Go and talk to Prosecutor Tommaseo. He's the one in charge of the kidnappings. You'll find him at the Palace of Justice at Montelusa."

Lo Curzio stood up; Montalbano did likewise.

"Tell me something — I'm curious," said the inspector. "How old are these women who work for you?"

"One is twenty-four, and the other two are in their forties. Mrs Eugenia Speciale, who works for Molisano, is close to retiring. Why do you ask?"

"Because the kidnapper's victims have all been in their thirties. Therefore, of the four women you mention, one is too young, and the other three are too old. So they should be safe. But who's going to tell a woman she has nothing to fear because she's no longer in her prime?"

Lo Curzio went out and the telephone rang.

"Ahh, Chief, 'ere'd a happen a be a Mr Urinale onna line 'oo wants a talk oigently wit' —"

"What did you say his name was?"

"Urinale."

Montalbano was damned if he was going to fall into Catarella's usual trap of mangling people's names.

"Let me talk to him."

"Inspector Montalbano? This is Giulio Uriale, and I'm manager of the Vigàta branch of the Banco Siculo. I need to confer with you urgently."

The inspector liked this use of the word "confer". He replied in kind.

"Presuming you're available, would it work for you to come here and confer with me at three-thirty this afternoon?"

"I thank you for your courtesy and concern."

What could he want?

The Banco Siculo had already been through one abduction and therefore probably had nothing more to worry about, relatively speaking, since the kidnapper seemed to change banks with each new abduction.

On the other hand, he thought, man's imagination in always thinking up new ways to be a pain in the arse seemed to know no limits.

When the inspector settled in at his usual table, Enzo bent down to say something in confidence.

"When you finally catch that bastard who gets off on kidnapping women, will you promise me something?"

"What, Enzo?"

"Will you let me have five minutes with him?"

"Don't be silly," Montalbano chided him.

"Do you know that my niece can no longer sleep at night?"

"We'll catch him, and he'll pay for his crimes, don't you worry about that."

He ate lightly, skipping the antipasti and ordering only a first and second course.

"You feeling OK?" Enzo asked, concerned.

"I'm fine, thanks, but since I have to be back at the office shortly . . ."

In the end he did take his customary stroll along the jetty, but once he reached the lighthouse at the end, rather than sit down on the flat rock, he turned on his heels and headed reluctantly back to land.

The bank manager Uriale came right on time.

He was the exact opposite of his professional counterpart Lo Curzio. Uriale was about sixty, nicely dressed and polite in manner and speech, and gave the impression of being a man you could trust.

"I should preface things, Inspector, by saying that I'm also here on behalf of Guido Sammartino of the Banca di Credito and Mario Zecchi of the Banca Cooperativa. They've assigned me the task of explaining our common problem to you."

"I'm all ears."

"Ever since a local television station named our three banks as the workplaces of the three women who were abducted, we have begun to notice a phenomenon that causes us great concern."

"And what would that be?"

"Numerous clients have closed their accounts with us. And we have discovered that, unfortunately, other account holders are getting ready to follow their example."

"For what reason?"

"Because there's been a wild rumour circulating, according to which these abductions will be followed by far more violent actions aimed at causing grave inconveniences to our banking institutions."

"I see."

"For the moment, at least, that's how things stand. But we fear they will get worse, despite our reassurances."

"And what would you like from me?"

"Before answering you, I must ask you a question myself, if you don't mind."

"Go right ahead."

"In what direction is your investigation heading?"

If only I knew! thought Montalbano. But he said in a firm voice: "In every direction possible."

Uriale seemed disappointed.

"So you're not ruling out that we may actually be looking at a series of actions intended to harm the banks?"

"At the current stage of our investigation, I can't rule that out. Even though, if we were to theorize a ranking of the different hypotheses, the 'banking lead' would not be among the top candidates."

"May I ask why?"

"First you must tell me the names of five towns or cities in the province with branches of the Banco Siculo."

"Montelusa, Fiacca, Sicudiana, Montereale, and Rivera."

"Have any of them had women employees abducted?"

"No, none."

"Now, please tell me, if this were really an attack on the banks, don't you think that all the branches would have been in some way affected?"

"Absolutely, yes."

"Then please listen to me. Repeat to your customers what I've just said to you. And advise them, if they're really set on leaving, to transfer their accounts to the Montelusa branch, which is barely four miles away."

The bank manager could barely refrain from kneeling down, tears in his eyes, and kissing the inspector's hand.

Fazio straggled back in around six. He looked fed up and discouraged.

"Nothing?"

"Nothing. A total waste of time. No travel agency booked any trips to the Canary Islands. One agent told me the Canaries nowadays are out of the loop. They're no longer fashionable."

"So what's the new fashion?"

"The latest fashion, especially for people without much money, is to go to one of the Greek islands, because it's really nice there and not at all expensive."

"Then Augello was right, I'm afraid. Apparently they did it all by computer."

But Fazio had something else to say.

"Chief, do you remember telling me to try to find out as much as I could about Di Carlo?"

"Of course."

"Everyone in town says the same things."

"Namely?"

"First, that he's a real womanizer, picks one up before he's dropped the last; and, second, that he's riddled with debts. He's always asking everyone for money, and gets along by creating new debts to pay off the old debts. Apparently he even asks the girls he has affairs with to lend him money. We should of course take these rumours with a grain of salt, but what's certain is that Di Carlo has debts, and big ones at that."

"And naturally this information reinforces your idea that he himself set fire to his shop."

"Well, two and two equals four, doesn't it, Chief?"

"Not always. To cite just one example, it could have been a loan shark who torched it."

"That's true, too," Fazio admitted.

The telephone rang.

"Ahh, Chief, 'ere'd be summon says 'is name's Carovania 'at wants a talk —"

"But is he on the line or is he here in person?"

"'E's 'ere poissonally in poisson, Chief."

"You know anyone named Carovania?" the inspector asked Fazio.

"No."

They had time to kill, so might as well . . . "Bring him in."

As soon as the man came in, Montalbano and Fazio immediately recognized Filippo Caruana, the salesman at Di Carlo's store. He seemed rather upset.

"I'm sorry if I . . . but . . ."

"What's going on?"

"Barely twenty minutes ago I saw Mr Di Carlo's car, the Porsche . . ."

"Are you sure it was his?"

"Absolutely certain."

"Where did you see it?"

"I was coming from Montelusa, and at Villaseta I turned inland to pay a visit to a girlfriend of mine, and along that road I saw the Porsche, in a secluded stretch with no houses. So I stopped and got out. It was locked, and there was nobody inside. Since the battery on my phone was dead, I thought I should come here to tell you in person."

"Let's waste no time," Montalbano said.

Caruana was driving so fast that Fazio had trouble keeping up with him.

When they got to Villaseta, they took a road that led into the countryside. After a while Caruana's car stopped and he got out. Montalbano and Fazio did the same.

"It was right here," said Caruana, practically speechless.

But there wasn't hide nor hair of the Porsche.

"We got here too late," said Fazio.

"When you went up to the car, were you able to tell whether it had just got there or had been there for a while?" Montalbano asked the youth.

Caruana answered at once.

"The engine was cold. I touched the bonnet to see."

The nearest house was about three hundred yards away.

Just to be thorough, they went to it.

But the peasant living there, a surly character who stank of stables, swore up and down that he hadn't seen any car corresponding to the description Caruana gave him.

"I'm sorry I made you waste so much time," Caruana said to Montalbano and Fazio, as he was leaving.

"No, you did exactly the right thing," the inspector replied. "And if you happen to see that car again, call us immediately. Don't worry about wasting our time."

During the drive home, Fazio said:

"Di Carlo's probably hiding out somewhere in the area."

"And we can't do anything about it," Montalbano retorted. "There are no charges pending against him, and on top of that, his sister didn't want to file a missing person's report. So set your heart at rest."

When they got back to the station, Montalbano was assailed by Catarella.

"Ahh, Chief! Mr Pitruzzo call'd wantin' a know if you was onna premisses an' so I said you wasn't. Then 'e wannit a know if I knew when you's comin' back an' so I said I din't know, insomuch as I din't know."

"And what did he say?"

"'E said 'at seein' as how an' considerin' 'e cou'n't talk t'yiz poissonally in poisson, he's gonna write yiz a litter."

Seeing as how and considering that he had nothing else left to do and it was late, Montalbano went home.

The first thing he did was to check and see what Adelina had made for him. Apparently his housekeeper had had a wave of inspiration.

There was a platter of seafood antipasti, enough for three people, and a big trayful of boiled langoustines, sheer essence of the sea, to be dressed with just olive oil, lemon, and salt.

It was a quiet evening. He laid the table on the veranda and had a feast. The telephone was polite and cooperative, waiting until he'd swallowed his last bite of langoustine before it started ringing.

At that hour, it was sure to be Livia.

"*Ciao, amore*," he said, raising the receiver to his ear.

"This is Commissioner Bonetti-Alderighi."

Shit. It was Hizzoner the C'mishner, and he'd called him *amore*! He didn't know what to do.

"I'm terribly sorry to bother you at home . . ."

My, my, how polite, how very nice Mr Commissioner was being! Apparently the Macannuco effect hadn't worn off yet.

"No bother at all, sir. What can I do for you?"

"Montalbano, I need you to console me."

To console him? Montalbano shuddered. What had got into the man? Did he want him to rock him in his arms or something?

CHAPTER
NINE

He imagined the gruesome scene: himself in half-light, sitting on the sofa in the commissioner's office, stroking Bonetti-Alderighi's head in his lap . . .

"I need some words of consolation," the commissioner clarified.

Montalbano breathed a big sigh of relief. Words of consolation were another matter entirely.

"I'm at your service."

"It's about the banks. You must have heard that there's a silly scare spreading among account holders who —"

"Yes, I've heard."

"Well, this evening, Tele Vigàta broadcast a feature in which the Honourable MP Cucciato viciously attacked me and you for having done nothing to allay the fears of the account holders and for not having followed the bank-sabotage lead in our investigation. Things being the way they are, I'm afraid I'm going to have to issue an official statement."

"I think you should."

"But please try to understand, first I would like to hear you say that you are absolutely certain, more than certain, that these kidnappings have nothing to do with the banks."

The inspector didn't hesitate for a second.

"I can confirm that, sir."

"And are you also willing to assume the full responsibility for your declaration?"

Ah, so the commissioner was protecting himself, covering his back. So if things took a bad turn, he could easily defend himself by laying the blame entirely on Montalbano.

"Of course."

"Your conviction is encouraging, and I greatly appreciate it. Because, you see, after they found those leaflets . . ."

What leaflets was he talking about? What was this? Better not let the commissioner know he knew nothing about them. For this reason he didn't ask for any explanation.

". . . in a few letter boxes, signed by a strange anti-bank organization, I became very, very worried. At any rate, thank you, and good night."

"And a good night to you, sir."

After putting down the receiver, he began cursing the saints.

Why the hell had he been so self-assured and decisive? And then that devious bastard of a commissioner came out with this business of the leaflets, only after the inspector had already compromised himself.

Certainly, from a logical point of view, the banks had nothing to do with any of this. But what if it really was some madman carrying out the abductions, someone

113

who hadn't the slightest idea where to find so much as the ghost of logic? And hadn't he, the inspector, indeed received a phone call from some unhinged nutcase claiming to speak on behalf of an organization called . . . called what? Ah, yes, the CABC, the Clandestine Anti-Bank Coalition?

Meanwhile, he was also furious at himself for another reason.

And he kept repeating to himself: *All these doubts, all these fears are crashing down on you because you're getting on in years, since old age undermines the self-assurance and certainties of youth.*

Then, all at once, it occurred to him that there was a way to calm down the account holders and allow Mr Commissioner to come out smelling like roses.

The inspector spent an hour on the veranda considering and reconsidering this idea from all possible angles.

And he came to the conclusion that he should put it into practice. After all, even if it turned out to be wrong, it would do no harm.

He was finally able to talk to Livia and go to bed.

He slept well, right through, and arrived at the office at nine o'clock sharp, fresh and rested.

"Cat, come into my office, there's something we need to work on together."

Upon hearing these words, Catarella blushed for joy, bolted out of his cubby-hole, and followed the inspector like a dog.

He was practically wagging his tail.

114

After entering the office, he planted himself at attention in front of the inspector's desk, standing as still as a statue.

"Catarella, did we register the phone numbers of all the calls we received during the night we spent together here at the station and ate bread and salami?"

"Assolutely, Chief."

"Then please go and get me the number for the caller who rang just after Fazio's call."

"I'll be right back, Chief."

Montalbano had no idea how Catarella did it, but in the twinkling of an eye, the switchboard operator was already standing in front of him again, still red in the face from the honour that had been given him, and handed him a little piece of paper.

"I writ the nummer onnit," he said.

The inspector dialled it.

"Commissioner's office," said a voice.

Montalbano hung up in a hurry, as though the receiver was burning his hand.

"Cat, you gave me the number of the commissioner's office."

"Oh, *matre santa!* Twaz a mistake! I'll be right back."

There was barely time to take a breath before Catarella rematerialized, holding another little piece of paper in his hand.

"Who's this?" asked a male voice.

"This is Inspector Montalbano, police. Who am I talking to?"

"You've reached the train station bar, Inspector."

Montalbano felt disappointed.

"How late do you stay open?"

"Till one in the morning."

So the phone call from the unhinged spokesman for the CABC had been made from that bar. Unhinged, perhaps, but certainly no fool.

So, what now? He had another idea.

"Cat, listen up."

"I'll lissen as up as I can, Chief."

"I want you to phone the five different banks in Vigàta, one at a time, tell them I want to talk to the bank manager, then put the call through to me after you do it, but first telling me which bank I'm talking to. Got that? That's not too hard, right?"

"Nah, Chief, I c'n do it if I 'ply myself."

Two minutes later the phone rang. Catarella seemed to be moving faster than the speed of light.

"Chief, iss the Banca di Tredito."

"Hello? Is this the manager of the Banca di Credito?"

"Yes, Inspector, what can I do for you?"

"I need a little information, which will remain confidential."

"All right, go ahead."

"I need to know whether there have been any recent firings or layoffs at your local branch."

"No, not that I can recall."

The inspector had more or less the same conversation with the manager of the Banco Siculo and the manager of the Banca Cooperativa.

The manager of the Credito Marittimo, on the other hand, gave a different answer to the question.

"Yes, unfortunately, four months ago I had to recommend — I repeat unfortunately — that an employee not be dismissed, but removed."

"What's the difference?"

"He wasn't exactly sacked; he was . . . how shall I say? . . . persuaded to resign."

"What had he done?"

"Until the moment he started displaying some very strange behaviour, he'd been a model employee."

"What kind of strange behaviour?"

"Well, one day he came to the bank in his pyjamas, another day he came in barefoot, a third time he brought a great big green umbrella that he insisted on keeping open over his desk, stuff like that . . . Until one day he received a certain Mrs Bianchini completely naked. The lady screamed and then fainted. It was sheer bedlam, know what I mean?"

"Yes, I understand. Could you tell me his name and how old he is?"

"His name is Arturo Sigonella, and he's a little over fifty."

"Married?"

"No, he lives alone."

"Any relatives?"

"None that I know of."

"Do you know where he lives?"

"No, but if you can wait for just a minute, I could ask a colleague of his who goes to see him every now and then."

"Please let me speak with him."

A minute went by, then a voice:

"Hello, Inspector? This is Michele Ferla."

"Has it been a while since you last paid a visit to Mr Sigonella?"

"Inspector, it's been a while since he started acting like a madman and calling me a slimy banker. I actually went to see him just last night, after not seeing him for a week, but, despite my insistence, he didn't want to open the door for me, and even said to me angrily, and repeatedly, that he no longer wanted to have anything to do with me."

"Did he give you any reason?"

"No, he just said disdainfully: 'I've had enough of talking to you, bankster!' And to think that he used to be —"

"Give me the address," said Montalbano, cutting him off. Taking it down, he thanked Michele Ferla and told Catarella not to make the last phone call on the list. Then he went into Fazio's office.

"Come with me. We'll take your car."

On the way, he told Fazio what he had in mind. And he explained to him how they should act.

Largo dei Mille was a rather central square. Fazio stopped outside the building marked number 4. It was a modern construction. Sigonella lived on the third floor, in the apartment just opposite the lift.

Fazio rang the doorbell. There was no reply. He rang again, keeping the doorbell pressed a long time. Finally they heard a voice say:

"There's no point in ringing, don't you realize?"

"Why not?" asked the inspector.

"Because there's nobody home."

Montalbano didn't lose his cool.

"Do you know when Mr Sigonella will be back?"

"If there's nobody here, nobody can answer your question."

Made perfect sense, you had to admit.

"OK. Tell you what. If nobody happens to see him, nobody should tell him that two gentlemen came here who agree entirely with everything involving his revolutionary activities and would like to join the CABC. Have a good day."

"Wait! Wait!" the voice said breathlessly.

"Bull's-eye!" Fazio whispered in admiration.

There was a loud jangling of keys and latches, and the door came open.

Before them stood a rather short man of about fifty, looking unkempt, dishevelled, and unshaven.

Montalbano bowed respectfully before him. "Are you the head of the CABC?"

Sigonella puffed out his chest.

"In person," he said.

"I'm Ragioniere Galasso, and this is my colleague Pozzi. He's a surveyor."

"Please come in."

The apartment was like its owner, dirty and in a state of disorder, and there was a stale, rancid smell in the air.

Sigonella showed them into a dusty sitting room, after turning the light on. The window was hermetically sealed, as all the others must also have been.

"How did you manage to find me?" asked Sigonella.

119

Fazio gave Montalbano a worried look. Would the inspector have a convincing lie ready to tell him? A lie at least good enough to convince a madman?

But the inspector told him a half-truth.

"It occurred to me that you might be the one, because I knew that you had suffered a terrible injustice from the bank where you used to work so devotedly for so many years. An injustice that cried out for revenge. And so we've come to let you know we're completely available."

"Well, you've come at just the right moment."

Sigonella looked all around to make sure there weren't any spies hiding in the room, then said in a soft voice:

"I've been able to print, right here at home, two thousand leaflets, but it's not easy for me to distribute them all by myself. Know what I mean? I have to take just a few at a time, put them in my pocket, go into unattended apartment buildings, and then slip the leaflets one by one into each tenant's letterbox . . ."

"We can give you a hand with that, if that's all right with you . . ."

"Of course it's all right with me."

"Where do you want them distributed?"

"In Vigàta."

Montalbano shook his head. "Mistake."

"Why?"

"Because you need to expand your area of operation. Extend the protest beyond Vigàta, make your way step by step to the big cities, all the way to the capitals — Rome, Berlin, London . . ."

120

Sigonella clapped his hands enthusiastically.

"I suggest we distribute them in Montelusa."

"But how will we do that? I don't have a car," Sigonella protested.

"We do. Let's not waste any time. Let's take those leaflets and go to Montelusa!"

They stacked the leaflets into the car and drove off. But ten minutes into their journey they had to stop because there was a roadblock set up by the carabinieri. Montalbano broke into a cold sweat. What if there was the same corporal who had arrested him just the other day?

He looked at Fazio, who was right beside him, and Fazio understood. He opened his door, got out, and went over to the marshal.

The inspector, meanwhile, was busy distracting Sigonella.

"This is a very dangerous situation we're in here. If the carabinieri discover our leaflets we're done for. So please stay calm. Stiff upper lip!"

The upshot of this was that he managed to make Sigonella start shaking all over in terror. Luckily Fazio returned.

"All taken care of."

Twenty minutes later, Fazio's car pulled up in the courtyard of Montelusa Central Police headquarters.

"Where are we?" asked Sigonella.

Montalbano felt terribly sorry for the poor bastard. But he had to continue his play-acting. He assumed a mysterious air.

"Please don't ask any questions. Get out of the car and go with Surveyor Pozzi, who will introduce you to some other friends."

Speechless, Sigonella obeyed.

"But is he the kidnapper?" asked the commissioner.

"Not on your life! Sigonella couldn't kidnap an ant! He's just a wretched nutcase who heard on TV that the three girls who were abducted worked at three different banks, got excited, invented the CABC, and now has been trying to distribute political leaflets he prints at home. He should be treated like the mental case he is. But you may be able to use his arrest to declare that the anti-bank lead was a red herring."

"I'm sorry, Montalbano, but what if we're faced with another abduction of a woman working at a bank? What do we do then?"

"Are you religious, sir?"

"Yes."

"Then I would advise you to say a novena to the Blessed Virgin and pray that doesn't happen."

"Ah, Chief, y'er back?"

"I'm back. Anything new?"

"Wha's new izzat Isspecter Augello tol' me to oigently tell 'im all oigentlike when you was back as soon you was back, an' since ya tol' me jess now 'at you was back —"

"Then tell 'im."

Then, turning to Fazio:

"You come, too."

122

Mimì appeared in a flash.

"You got something for me?" Montalbano asked.

"Yeah," said Mimì, yawning.

"Didn't you sleep last night?"

"Not much."

Another yawn.

"Mimì, maybe it would be best if you went home and got a little more sleep."

"No, no, it's just because last night I took a girl out to dinner and we stayed up late."

"Mimì, I haven't got time to listen to reports of your amorous exploits."

"But this is a service report I'm trying to make!"

"Then speak and try not to yawn so much," Montalbano said, yawning. "See? Yawning is contagious."

"The girl in question is named Anna Bonifacio. I had an affair with her four years ago."

"Imagine that!" the inspector exclaimed ironically.

Augello pretended not to notice.

"Yesterday I called her, invited her out, she hemmed and hawed, and then finally accepted."

"And what does this woman do for a living?"

"Well, that's where my move was a stroke of genius. She works at the same bank as Luigia Jacono."

Montalbano and Fazio pricked up their ears. "And what did she tell you?"

"I'll try to keep it brief. She told me two things that seem important to me. The first is that on the first of May this year — which was a holiday — Anna went with a friend of hers to Taormina, where they happened to see a couple kissing passionately inside a fancy car.

When the two people got out of the car, Anna, to her great surprise, recognized the woman as Luigia. And she also recognized the man, because he was a customer at the bank. And do you know who this man was?"

"Marcello Di Carlo," said Montalbano.

Mimì got upset, since the inspector always ruined his surprises.

"Well, if you know everything already, there's no need for me to say any more," he said, frowning and looking resentful.

Montalbano tried to defuse the situation. He hadn't purposely tried to upset him; the name had simply come out by itself.

"Come on, Mimì, don't be childish. I don't know anything. I swear I was going by sense of smell."

"So the last affair he had, before the one with the girl in Lanzarote, was with Luigia?" Fazio intervened.

"So it would seem," said Augello. "And there's more. But, before telling you two, I want some iron-clad assurance that our dear Inspector Montalbano, here present — the Eternal Father of all police inspectors — doesn't already know it; otherwise, I'll just shut up and let him talk."

"Mimì. Stop being such a pain in the arse. What, you want it in writing that I don't know any of what you're saying?"

"Oh, all right . . . So, around mid-June, the current account Di Carlo had at the bank was blocked by a court injunction, after a complaint by a creditor. The

124

bank alerted Di Carlo, who didn't even protest. A week later the injunction was lifted."

"Apparently he'd managed to find the money to pay off his debt," said Fazio.

"Let me finish," Augello said impatiently. "Naturally, the creditor's name was never mentioned. But, purely by chance, Anna found out who it was. The person who'd blocked his account was Luigia Jacono."

This time, Mimì got the desired effect of surprise he'd been seeking. Montalbano and Fazio were momentarily speechless.

"And this explains the young woman's behaviour when I spoke to her," said the inspector. "I got the impression that she'd thought she was the only one who'd been abducted and subjected to that torture, and that she thought she knew the reason for it. But now we know the reason, too. Luigia believed she was the victim of a delayed vendetta on Di Carlo's part. Carried out not by Di Carlo himself, but by a hired hand. Which is a step forward for us, though it rather complicates the whole picture."

"Meaning?" asked Augello.

"Meaning that Luigia recognized the car at the side of the road as Di Carlo's Porsche Cayenne."

"So then why didn't she step on the accelerator?"

"Maybe the kidnapper stood in front of her car and she didn't have the nerve to run him over."

"Wait a second," said Fazio. "If that's the way it is, does it mean the two prior kidnappings were also ordered by Di Carlo, though using a stolen car? And for what purpose?"

Fazio's argument was not to be taken lightly. And in fact Montalbano preferred not to answer his question.

CHAPTER
TEN

"But we can also venture a completely different hypothesis," Augello cut in. "Which is that there are actually two kidnappers. The first goes about his business using a stolen car, but then these two abductions give Di Carlo the idea to get revenge on Luigia by abducting her likewise. That way we'll be led to think it's a third kidnapping by the same culprit when in fact it's a totally separate case. And since he can't carry out the action himself, he hires an accomplice to do it, lending him his car."

"Mind if I venture yet another hypothesis?" asked Montalbano.

"What would that be?" said Mimì.

"That would be that the kidnapper is always the same person, but what has changed is that now he's using Di Carlo's car, which is in his possession either because he's stolen it or because Di Carlo can't use it. In fact, as things now stand, Di Carlo is nowhere to be found, either because he wants to scam the insurance company or because he is not free to move about."

Fazio, feeling confused, buried his face in his hands. "We're in a labyrinth," he said.

"But we should be able to find our way out of it without getting too discouraged, even if so many of our tries come to nothing," Montalbano commented. Then, turning to Fazio:

"Find out if Luigia's still in the hospital," he said.

Fazio picked up the phone and dialled.

"Yes, she's still there," he said when he'd finished. "They're releasing her tomorrow morning."

"I'm going to question her this afternoon. Fazio, be sure to be back here at three-thirty. We'll take my car. See you after lunch."

Once again he ate lightly at the trattoria. Enzo immediately got worried.

"You feeling all right, Inspector?"

"I'm feeling fine, don't worry. It'll pass. I'll be better soon."

Since he didn't have much time, he took his walk along the jetty at a marching pace.

At half-past three he headed to Montelusa with Fazio. Who'd brought with him a lawyer's-style briefcase.

"What have you got in the briefcase?" the inspector asked him.

"What I need to write a report."

"You don't need to write a report."

"Are we going to do any play-acting?"

"No, we're not going to do any play-acting."

"Am I supposed to be a witness?"

"No."

"So what do you need me for?"

"I need you to keep me from getting lost in the hospital."

Fazio just gazed at him, wide-eyed in wonder.

When Montalbano walked into the room with Fazio he had the impression that the girl wasn't the least bit surprised. Apparently she'd been expecting just such a visit.

Luigia had recovered nicely. She had good colour, and above all seemed no longer agitated.

The inspector sat in the chair at the foot of her bed. Fazio remained standing.

"How do you feel today?"

"Much better, thank you. I've been told I can finally go home tomorrow."

"How's your father? Is he all right?"

"Yes, he's feeling better, especially since I spoke to him on the phone. I didn't tell him I'd been abducted; that would upset him too much. I just told him I'd had a minor accident."

Montalbano now had two roads before him for continuing the interrogation: the roundabout route, slowly zeroing in on what interested him most; or going straight to the point with questions that would trip up the person being interrogated.

With Luigia he decided to take the second route. During their first encounter, the girl had shown herself to be a pretty tough nut to crack.

"Did the fact of learning that yours wasn't the only recent case of abduction, but the third in a series of abductions, help you to recover from the trauma?"

"Why should that have helped me recover?"

Luigia had parried the blow readily. Montalbano was starting to like her.

It really was like a fencing match with her. She knew she was at his level, and had no need to overdo it.

"Luigia, you are very intelligent and quick to understand things."

"Thank you."

"But you often pretend not to understand. Let me speak to you quite frankly, to avoid any misunderstandings. Let me begin by saying that I consider this conversation between us personal and confidential, and it will remain such because it will not be written down. Is that clear?"

"Yes."

"All I want you to do is answer my questions sincerely. Is that all right with you?"

"Yes, that's fine with me."

She said these words in a confident tone. The inspector's statement had convinced her.

"During the period between April of this year and June, did you have an affair with Marcello Di Carlo?"

As the last thing the woman was expecting was a question so direct and precise, her face first turned pale then immediately fire red. She didn't answer.

"Luigia, you have nothing to be ashamed of. Unfortunately, in spite of my better nature I'll have to ask you still other questions of this sort, because it's my job. So, please answer the question."

Her reply was barely a breath. "Yes," she said.

"Did Di Carlo ask you to lend him money?"

"Yes."

"How much?"

"Fifty thousand euros."

"Did you agree?"

"Yes."

She was about to say something else, but then stopped, undecided. Then she seemed to summon her courage and make up her mind.

"He begged me with tears in his eyes," she said.

"Do you remember by any chance when he told you he intended to break off your relationship?"

"On the fifth of June. It would be hard for me to forget the date."

"What did he say?"

"He said he'd fallen in love with another woman."

"Did he tell you her name?"

"No."

"And you haven't managed to find out by other means?"

"No."

"So you still don't know who this other woman is?"

"No, I don't, and I don't care."

"When Di Carlo told you your affair was over, how did you react? Did you passively accept it, or did you . . ."

Luigia practically covered her face with the sheet, feeling suddenly embarrassed.

"I reacted badly. I was petty and mean."

"Tell me what you did."

"I'm so ashamed."

Montalbano came to her aid.

"Did you ask him to return the money you'd lent him?"

"Yes."

"And what did he do?"

"He said he couldn't."

"So you had his bank account blocked?"

"Yes. I had a copy of the wire transfer as proof of the loan, and I turned to a friend of mine who's a judge. But since there were only thirty thousand euros in his account, it was blocked. Just a few days later, however, fifty thousand euros were wired in from the Credito Marittimo, and so his account was unblocked."

"Let's move on to the abduction. The car you saw parked at the side of the road with the bonnet up: was it Marcello Di Carlo's Porsche Cayenne?"

"Yes."

"Since it would have been logical to fear some kind of reaction on Di Carlo's part, why did you pull over?"

"But at that moment I wasn't fearing any violent reaction on Mar — on Di Carlo's part!"

"Why not?"

"Because enough time had gone by, and I didn't really think, and still don't think, he was capable of violent behaviour."

"How tall was the man who abducted you?"

"About five foot eleven, I would say."

"And how tall is Di Carlo?"

Luigia looked at him uncomprehendingly.

"Why are you asking me that? Have you never had a chance to meet him?"

"He's gone missing and can't be located. Please answer my question."

"About five foot eight."

"You've already said the abductor seemed like an older man."

"Yes."

"So you were immediately aware that that man was not Di Carlo?"

"Of course."

"Was he sweating?"

"Yes. He smelled bad."

"The last time we spoke you told me that the whole time you were with him, the man didn't once open his mouth. Do you confirm that?"

"Yes."

"Was Di Carlo in the habit of lending his car?"

"No. He was very jealous of his possessions. The only person he made exceptions for was his friend Giorgio Bonfiglio."

"Do you know this Bonfiglio well?"

"If one is with Marcello Di Carlo, one inevitably gets to know Bonfiglio, unfortunately."

"Why 'unfortunately'?"

"I really don't like him."

"Is there any specific reason?"

Before speaking, Luigia took a deep breath.

"On the afternoon of June the fifth, after leaving the bank, I went to Marcello's house, where he was supposed to be waiting for me. But he wasn't there. In his place was Bonfiglio. Who immediately tried to hit on me, putting his hands all over me. Over an hour later, Marcello finally arrived and Bonfiglio left. Not long after, Marcello told me he wanted to leave me. So I came to the conclusion that they had conspired together. If the plan worked, Marcello would have caught me in Bonfiglio's arms, made a scene, and called me a slut. And he would have had a reason for postponing repayment of the loan."

"What was the nature of your encounters with Bonfiglio?"

"Aside from that one afternoon, he was always with Marcello when I saw him. We would often go out to dinner together."

"And would Bonfiglio come alone?"

"No, he would bring along a girlfriend about my age, very pretty, by the name of Silvana."

"Do you know her surname?"

"No. Bonfiglio introduced her to me simply as his girlfriend. But Silvana didn't come to our last two dinners together."

"Did these two dinners take place in early June?"

"Yes. Noticing she wasn't there, I asked Bonfiglio about her, but he answered me evasively on both occasions."

"Did Di Carlo ask Bonfiglio about Silvana?"

"Not in my presence, no."

"Can you tell me anything else about this Silvana?"

"She's a very beautiful girl. She had very long hair, with a big streak dyed purple. She didn't talk much about herself. She had a job at some kind of business consulting firm, but I could be wrong."

"Now, try to think carefully. Based on what you have told me about the complicity between Di Carlo and Bonfiglio, and the fact that Di Carlo never lent his car to anyone except him, when you saw that the person beside the Porsche was not Di Carlo but someone else, did you have any sense of who it might be?"

Luigia answered the question, but her reply was not what the inspector had been expecting.

"I'm not going to say the name you're indirectly suggesting to me and want to hear me say."

"Will you tell me why?"

"Because I can't be absolutely certain."

"But did you think, even if only for a second, that it might be that person?"

"Yes."

"Merely because he was tinkering with the engine of the Porsche?"

"No, it was also his height, his gait . . ."

"So, what is the reason for your uncertainty?"

"Inspector, in order to press the chloroform pad against my face, that man had to hold me tight from behind. His only moves were ones he couldn't avoid making. I'm more than convinced that Bonfiglio would not have behaved so correctly. And he would certainly have taken advantage of me while I was unconscious."

"Thank you for your cooperation. Your testimony is very valuable to me," said Montalbano, standing up.

"This Luigia impressed me quite a bit," said Fazio as they were driving back to Vigàta. "She only says things

135

she's sure about. She doesn't let her imagination run away with her."

"Are you telling me — with a good dose of Vaseline to make it easier — that Luigia will never officially admit that the man who abducted her could have been Bonfiglio?"

"Well, yes. But do you really think it was him? After all this time?"

"People don't always act according to logic and timing. Anyway, he's got a lot stacked against him. The fact that Di Carlo would lend him the car, that the abductor was an older man, five foot eleven, and that he didn't say a word to Luigia, who would have recognized his voice . . . And there's another thing, too: he abducts Luigia as a favour to Di Carlo, who he's hand in glove with, but he also has a personal motive: to avenge himself on the woman who resisted his advances."

"But then, as Luigia said, he should have raped her."

"Don't forget what Augello told us about him: he's a poker player, a master bluffer. Raping her would have given us a card leading us straight to him."

"So how do you want us to proceed?"

"It would be a mistake to question him about the kidnapping. Summon him for nine-thirty tomorrow morning, and if he asks why, tell him we want to know more about Di Carlo."

"All right."

Montalbano sat there for a moment in thoughtful silence. Then he asked:

"Listen, do you know anyone who works at the Credito Marittimo?"

"No, but I can probably manage to find someone."

"I want to know who sent the wire for fifty thousand euros to Luigia Jacono during the month of June."

"Let me get something straight. You're of the opinion that Di Carlo got Bonfiglio to kidnap the girl so that we would think it was the third in a series?"

"Yes, that's the way I see it now."

"So that means we still have to solve the problem of who carried out the first two kidnappings?"

"Unfortunately, yes."

After he'd eaten the *pasta 'ncasciata* and the mullet with Adelina's special sauce, he cleared the table on the veranda and phoned Livia. When she asked him how the kidnapping investigation was coming along, he brought her up to date and even went into the details. Livia's reaction caught him by surprise.

"Don't you think the conclusion you've reached is a bit far-fetched? If you ask me, the third abduction was carried out by the same person who did the first two."

"But, Livia —"

"Look, Salvo, it was you yourself who told me that the third abduction was carried out using exactly the same method as the first two."

"So what?"

"So if you never made this method public, how could Di Carlo and Bonfiglio have known about it? And there can only be one answer to this question."

"And what would that be?"

137

"They can't have known unless they were the authors of the two prior kidnappings. But what would be their purpose for doing that?"

Montalbano remained silent for a moment, mulling over what Livia had just said. Then he replied:

"There must be a reason."

"Yes, but what?"

"To muddy the waters and put us on the wrong track."

"I don't understand."

"Instead of immediately abducting Luigia, they grabbed two other girls to create this mysterious figure of a serial kidnapper who doesn't really exist, just to distract any suspicion away from themselves. An elaborate plan like that, moreover, would be perfectly in keeping with a mentality like Bonfiglio's."

Livia seemed convinced. They spoke for a little while longer, then wished each other a good night. Montalbano stayed out on the veranda for another hour or so, thinking about how to proceed with Bonfiglio.

It was just past midnight when he went to bed.

It was a good thing he hadn't wasted any time watching a late-night movie on TV, as he often did, because he was woken up just before six by the phone.

A phone call at that hour could mean only one thing.

So true was this, that some years earlier he had coined a little adage, or whatever you might want to call it, for his own personal use and enjoyment:

A phone call at daybreak means murder or housebreak.

"Wha' was ya doin', Chief, sleepin'?"

There was fear in Catarella's voice as he asked the question.

"No, Cat, I was playing ping-pong."

Montalbano's retort had come out in a harsh, rude tone of voice, but he hadn't taken into account that for Catarella it might seem perfectly normal for someone to be playing ping-pong at six o'clock in the morning.

"Oh, sorry f' innaruptin' yer game."

"Not to worry, I was playing by myself."

"Man, Chief, y'er rilly sum'in'! How do ya do it?"

"I run from one end of the table to the other while the ball is in the air. So, what did you have to tell me?"

"'At Gallo's on 'is way ta get yiz."

Montalbano hung up without asking for an explanation. Gallo wouldn't take more than ten minutes to drive from Vigàta to Marinella, so there wasn't much time to get ready.

He showered, shaved, dressed, and drank coffee at an accelerated pace, moving about like a character in a silent movie. Gallo only had to wait five minutes.

The inspector barely had time to get in the car before Gallo shot off like a rocket, siren blaring.

"Turn that shit off."

Gallo obeyed reluctantly.

"Do you know what's going on?" Montalbano asked him.

"Yessir, they found a dead body, apparently. Fazio's at the scene."

Gallo turned onto a road that led into the countryside, inland, behind the town.

It was an area where not a square inch of land wasn't cultivated for farming, and in addition to the farms the landscape was dotted with houses and cottages of people who drove into town to work.

All these houses and cottages had, of course, been illegally constructed, since it was an area unauthorized for building.

And this was why one saw, here and there, constructions abandoned halfway, because every so often the local authorities would put a freeze on a project because the owner hadn't been sly or clever enough to come to an arrangement in advance.

It was right next to one of these small houses, fully constructed but left unplastered on the outside, with only holes for doors and windows, that the inspector spotted Fazio's car.

There was another car parked beside it. Gallo pulled up, and Montalbano got out.

The air was pure, cool, and clean, and it promised to be a cooperative, peaceful morning.

Fazio popped out from the opening that would one day become the front door, followed by a man of about fifty, well dressed, short, pudgy, bespectacled, and with a pink, practically hairless face.

If he'd been wearing a frock, he would have made a perfect priest.

Fazio introduced him.

The man turned out to be Angelo Rizzo, a lawyer. He was the one who had discovered the corpse and called the police.

140

CHAPTER
ELEVEN

"Do you live around here?"

It was a logical question, and yet it seemed to trigger a nervous reaction in the lawyer, who all at once started hopping in the air on his little feet.

He looked a wind-up doll.

"Well, no . . . however . . . I live on Corso Matteotti."

Corso Matteotti was a street in central Vigàta. It had no connection whatsoever to the place where they all were at that moment.

"I'm sorry, but what were you doing in this area at the crack of dawn?"

The hopping became almost frantic.

"Actually . . . well . . . it's like this . . . of course . . . So, on my way back from Palermo . . ."

Montalbano wouldn't let up.

"But coming back from Palermo one doesn't pass —"

"Yes, of course, this road isn't . . . but, you see, yesterday evening, on my way back from Palermo, I rang up a woman I know — on the spur of the moment, just to talk — a woman I know who lives around here, and so . . . She told me her husband had left her and she was in need of some comfort . . . and so . . . I informed my wife that I wouldn't be back till the morning, and so . . ."

Montalbano decided to be a pain. "And so what?"

Rizzo the lawyer started sweating.

"And so . . . one thing led to another . . ."

The inspector decided to drop it.

"I see," he said.

The lawyer then brought his face so close to Montalbano's that the inspector thought the man wanted to kiss him. "I'm rather well known, actually. I hold an important . . . If you could manage to keep my name out of this . . ."

"I'll do what I can. So why did you go into this house?"

At this point the lawyer suddenly got a tic, which consisted of him stretching his neck out and then jerking his head quickly to the left.

"I realized I'd forgotten to . . . to put . . . to put my . . . underpants back on. There. I couldn't very well go home and undress . . . If my wife happened to . . . how would I ever explain . . . And so I took a pair from my suitcase, got out of the car, and . . ."

"Why not just put them on in your car?"

"I tried, but it was so cramped . . . I got out, went into the first room, but then, just to be safe, went further inside and that's when I saw . . . the mummy."

The mummy?

Montalbano, speechless, looked over at Fazio.

"Yeah, because the body's all wrapped up . . . as you'll see for yourself," said Fazio. Then he added: "I've already alerted everyone."

142

"So . . . if I could perhaps go . . . before . . ." the lawyer said.

"I've got his address and telephone number," Fazio cut in.

"All right, then, you can go."

"Thank you, thank you so much," said the lawyer, bowing repeatedly to the inspector.

After which he practically ran away, got into his car, turned on the ignition, and drove off at high speed.

"Shall we go inside?" asked Fazio. They went inside.

The room was still lacking floor tiles, but to make up for it they walked on a layer of old newspapers, rags, used condoms, hypodermic needles, empty cans, leftover pizza, empty water and beer bottles, and puddles of urine . . .

The second room was no different from the first but for the fact that, towards the back, there was a sort of long, narrow package wrapped in cellophane.

"Who knows how long this body's been here without anyone deigning to let us know?" said Fazio.

"Are you surprised?" the inspector replied. "Just last summer I happened to see on TV some footage of a corpse on a beach with people all around it swimming and playing in the water as though it was nothing. There's no longer any respect for life, and you expect people to respect death?"

Since there wasn't anything for them to do in there, they went back outside. The inspector lit a cigarette and sat down to wait patiently for the circus to arrive.

★ ★ ★

The first to arrive was the coroner, Dr Pasquano, whose car led the way for the mortuary vehicle and its two undertakers.

The doctor got out of his car, cursing, slammed the door, and didn't bother to greet anyone.

"Did you by any chance lose at poker last night, Doctor?" Montalbano enquired.

"Don't get in my face first thing in the morning. It's way too dangerous. Where's this body?"

"Follow me," said Fazio.

They came back out some ten minutes later. Pasquano opened the door to his car, got in, and closed it again. Which meant that he didn't want to be disturbed by anyone.

"Did he say anything?" the inspector asked Fazio.

"Nothing. He didn't once open his mouth."

Montalbano walked over to Pasquano's car and tapped on the window. The doctor lowered it.

"What the fuck do you want?"

"Doctor, every time I see you, your exquisite politeness moves me to tears."

"Ah, so we're feeling poetic this morning? It often happens in one's later years. All right, then. What would you like to know, my old friend?"

Montalbano didn't return the jab about ageing. "What did you make of it?"

"Very well wrapped."

"Aside from the wrapping."

"Based on the little I was able to see, the man died a few days ago; this is not a fresh corpse."

144

"Any idea whether it was a natural or a violent death?"

"If you had just made up your mind to buy a good pair of glasses, as I've been advising you to do for some time, you would have noticed that the corpse has a nice round hole under the throat."

"Caused by what?"

"In my opinion — and it's only an impression, mind you — that hole is an exit wound."

Montalbano's face darkened.

"So if that's an exit wound, it means he was killed with a gunshot to the nape?"

"I'm pleased to see that at least part of your brain is still functioning. Now get out of here. You've already bothered me well beyond the limit."

And he raised the window. Montalbano went over to Fazio to tell him what he'd just learned from Pasquano.

Fazio turned pensive.

"That kind of murder bears the Mafia's signature," he remarked. "But this is the first time I've seen the Mafia wrap up a body after they liquidated the victim. What need was there to pack him up like that?"

"The whole thing makes no sense to me either," said the inspector. "But tell me something. Did you notice that there's a hole at the bottom of the corpse's throat?"

"No, I didn't," replied Fazio.

Montalbano heaved a sigh of relief. So he didn't need glasses yet after all. Pasquano had spotted the wound because he had an expert eye.

There was a moment of silence, then Fazio spoke.

"If it really is a Mafia murder, then this body could be . . ."

". . . Di Carlo's?" said Montalbano, finishing his thought. "It's a reasonable assumption."

"Yeah, I agree. Except that, like you, I don't understand the need to wrap it up."

He glanced at his watch. What with one thing and another it was already a few minutes past eight. He could go now and leave Fazio behind, but there was something specific he wanted to know from Forensics.

"Phone Bonfiglio and tell him our appointment has been pushed back to eleven o'clock."

Fazio did as he was told, but then, still holding his phone against his ear, said: "Bonfiglio is sorry, but wants to know if we can postpone the appointment till tomorrow at the same hour."

"OK."

Forensics finally arrived in two cars full of men and equipment. The chief of the squad was somebody Montalbano didn't recognize.

"Who's that?"

"Briguglio," replied Fazio. "He's a deputy inspector."

"What's he like?"

"He's manageable."

Briguglio came up and introduced himself, and Fazio led the group into the house.

The inspector had to wait half an hour before Fazio reappeared.

"In Briguglio's opinion, the body was brought here four days ago," Fazio reported.

"How did he determine that?"

"Because on the floor under the body was a page from a newspaper from five days ago."

This was exactly what he had wanted to know. "Any news of Prosecutor Tommaseo?"

"No. As usual, he probably ended up crashing into a pole or driving into a ditch."

Tommaseo was famous for driving worse than a sleep-walking drug addict.

"You know what I say? I'm sick of hanging around. I'm going to get Gallo to drive me to the office."

Try as Gallo might to get the squad car to achieve liftoff, it was already past nine by the time they got to the station.

"Is Inspector Augello in?"

"'E was — in, I mean — but then 'e got a phone call an' so 'e went out."

"Do you know where he went?"

"No, sir, Chief."

"Well, when he gets back, tell him to come to my office."

Not knowing what else to do, the inspector reluctantly started signing a few of the hated documents piled up on his desk.

Just when his arm was beginning to ache from too many signatures, Mimì Augello knocked at the door.

"So where were you?"

"I went out to get a coffee and have a chat with Anna Bonifacio, the girl who works with Luigia Jacono."

"Given how long you were out, you must have ordered more than just a coffee."

"What can I say? I had to thank her for the favour she'd done me."

"What favour was that?"

"Well, since she told me that Di Carlo's debt to La Jacono was paid off by a wire transfer from the Credito Marittimo, I asked her whether she knew anyone at that bank and —"

"You know what, Mimì? I'd had the same idea and asked Fazio to look into it, but —"

"But this time I got there first."

"Did you get the name?"

"Yes, Anna found out who it was and told me."

"And who is it?"

"How come you can't just guess this time?"

"Want me to try?"

"Go ahead and try."

"The girl from Lanzarote."

"Unfortunately you're wrong. If it had been her, we would now know her name, address, and phone number!"

"So tell me, then."

"Giorgio Bonfiglio."

Montalbano didn't seem too shocked by this revelation.

"Aren't you surprised?" asked Mimì.

"Not really. They're such close friends . . . In fact, I also think that, sometime in late June or early July, Bonfiglio gave him even more money."

"What makes you think that?"

"If Di Carlo didn't have a cent to his name, where'd he get the money to go and live it up in Lanzarote?"

"Want me to try and find out whether Bonfiglio sent any other wires to Di Carlo around that time?"

148

"If you can."

"I can try."

The telephone rang.

"Ahh, Chief, 'ere'd a happen a be a soitan Mr Quallalera onna line oigently wantin' a talk t'yiz."

He didn't know anyone by the name of Quallalera. But he had nothing else to do, so . . .

"OK."

"Inspector Montalbano? This is Giulio Caldarera. I wanted to tell you about something strange that happened."

He had a fresh voice, that of a young man. "Go ahead."

"I live in Vigàta. This morning I went out to pay a visit to my brother, who has been ill for days with the flu. He lives in a small house in the Ficarra district. Do you know it?"

"Yes. Isn't that where Mr Jacono lives?"

"Exactly. It's in the same district, but my brother lives at the opposite end."

"Where Riccobono lives?"

"Yes, I can see you know the area well. So, on my way there, just before the crossroads, at the side of the road I saw the car of someone I know, and a man pulling a folding bicycle out of the boot. And just now, as I was passing the same spot, I saw the same car in flames and no sign of the man."

"Are you still there?"

"Yes."

"Please wait for us. We're on our way." Then, turning to Mimì:

"You come with me."

"To do what?"

"A young man just called to report a car that's been set on fire. And since you're the specialist in torched cars . . ."

They got to the scene of the crime, as Catarella might have called it, in a flash, since Gallo was driving. Caldarera got out of his car as soon as he saw them, and started walking towards them.

He was a youth of about twenty, dark and handsome, with a bright smile and a likeable, intelligent manner.

All that was left of the torched car, which was just barely off the road, was a charred carcass still giving off a few wisps of smoke.

"They must have set fire to it just after I passed," said the lad. "By the time I returned, it was already burning itself out."

Montalbano didn't bother to go and look at the car from up close. That wasn't what interested him.

"Did you get a good look at the man who was pulling the bike out of the boot?" he asked the youth.

"I did see him, but if you ask me what he looked like I wouldn't be able to tell you."

"Why not?"

"Because he was wearing a cap pulled down to his eyebrows, dark sunglasses, and had a scarf wrapped around his mouth as though he had a cold . . ."

Montalbano and Augello exchanged a glance. That was exactly how the kidnapper covered himself to avoid being recognized.

"Can you tell me anything else?"

150

"By the way he moved, he didn't seem very young to me. Too bad, though."

"Too bad about what?"

"About the car he torched. I'm really into cars and I know how much —"

"What kind of car was it?" Augello interrupted him impatiently.

"A Porsche Cayenne. It's the only one in Vigàta."

"And do you know who it belongs to?"

"Of course. Marcello Di Carlo, who has an electronics shop —"

"Didn't it seem strange to you that it wasn't Di Carlo driving it?" the inspector asked.

"I just assumed he'd let him borrow it."

They thanked the youth, Augello alerted Forensics, and they went back to the station.

On the drive back, the inspector got Fazio on the phone. "What point are you at?"

"I'm on my way back."

"So are we. We went to see a car that was torched. It was Di Carlo's Porsche."

"What do you think that means?"

"It may mean that there won't be any more kidnappings. Unless the guy steals another car and keeps abducting women."

Naturally, since Gallo was driving, they got back to the station five minutes before Fazio, who, upon arriving, said:

"There's a new development."

"Good, we need one," said Montalbano. "We've been getting a little bogged down in this mess."

"The forensics people demanded that the undertakers unwrap the body before taking it away."

"Why?"

"They want to test the cellophane for fingerprints."

"Oh, right! As if the killer would be stupid enough not to have used gloves!" said Augello.

"Anyway," Fazio resumed, "I was able to get a good look at the naked corpse, and from up close. It's a man of about forty, pretty well groomed. But the important thing is that he has a Z-shaped scar under his left shoulder blade."

"That should help to identify him," said Augello.

"I've got an opinion on that, as far as that goes," said Fazio.

"Let's hear it," Montalbano said, prodding him.

"Since he'd been dead for a while, the face on the body was rather deteriorated, but still, when I was able to see it after they removed the cellophane, it reminded me of someone I'd seen in a photograph. And you saw it, too," he said to Montalbano.

"I did?" the inspector asked incredulously.

"You certainly did."

"Where?"

"At Di Carlo's house. There were two framed photos in his study. And in both, we see this person with an elderly couple, perhaps his father and mother."

"Yes, now I remember," said the inspector, "though only vaguely."

152

"I'm sorry, but didn't you guys say he had a sister?" Augello cut in. "We can ask her."

"No, because, then, if it's not Di Carlo . . ." said the inspector.

"We could ask Bonfiglio, who must surely know whether Di Carlo has a scar like that," Fazio suggested.

"I think it's best, for now, to keep Bonfiglio out of this. We can play that card when we interrogate him," said the inspector.

"That leaves only Luigia Jacono," said Mimì.

Montalbano looked over at Fazio.

"I get it," said Fazio. "It's my turn. But, if you don't mind, I'll call her from my office."

While waiting, Mimì Augello took out the newspaper he had in his jacket pocket and started reading it. Montalbano, for his part, decided to clean up his desk drawers, but upon opening the first one, got immediately discouraged. It was a proper emporium, with everything imaginable: ballpoint pens, letters, stamps, pencils, notebooks, outdated calendars, newspaper clippings, memos, a compass, and even a shirt he thought he'd lost. He closed it again without touching anything and stared at the wall in front of him.

Finally Fazio returned.

"Yes, it's definitely him. Luigia Jacono says Di Carlo had a scar just like that one."

"Did she ask you why you wanted to know?"

"Yes. And so I told her the truth."

"And how'd she react?"

"She started crying."

CHAPTER
TWELVE

The inspector glanced at his watch. It was getting so late that he was in danger of finding his customary trattoria closed.

Still, there were a few things he wanted to clear up before the lunch break.

"The fact that Di Carlo was murdered rules out a few possible hypotheses but suggests a few others," he began. "However, before saying anything else, I want you both to be clear that nobody must know, for the moment, that we've identified the body. I want to see how Bonfiglio reacts when I tell him."

Then, turning to Fazio:

"The murder of Di Carlo completely nullifies your hypothesis that it was he himself who set fire to his shop before disappearing, so he could scam the insurance company. Do you agree?"

"Yes."

"Moreover," the inspector continued, "the fact that he was killed a few days after returning from Lanzarote rules out that he could have been the person who organized Luigia's abduction. Do you both agree?"

"Yes," Mimì and Fazio replied in unison.

154

"So, then, the question now is: who killed Di Carlo, and why?"

"You still don't think it could have been the Mafia, since Di Carlo had refused to pay the racket?" asked Fazio.

"The Mafia has never kidnapped anybody for not paying the racket. They either set fire to their shop or place of business, or else kill the owner before everyone's eyes, to set an example. They would never hide the body away, let alone wrap it up in cellophane."

"Do you have any idea why anyone would want to wrap up a corpse like that?" asked Augello.

"There is one possible explanation. The sheets of wrapping not only enveloped the whole corpse from head to toe; they were also carefully closed shut, sealed, in fact, with tape."

"Why, do you think?"

"By sealing the sheets of cellophane in this fashion, they prevented any air from circulating and any smell from wafting out. You could keep a corpse like that in your own house, or anywhere at all, without anyone ever smelling the rot."

"I'm sorry," said Mimì, "but why would the killer keep his victim at home instead of getting rid of the body as quickly as possible?"

"Mimì, if I could answer your question, I would be well on the way to solving the case. Let me think about that a little. For now, let's go and have some lunch. We'll meet here at four."

The fact that he'd left the house early that morning and had been out in the open air for so long had stirred up

155

in him the sort of wolflike hunger that had begun to seem a thing of the past. After witnessing the immense satisfaction with which he'd eaten his pasta in squid ink, Enzo set before him two second courses: the usual red mullet, and a dish of fried squid so crisp and clean they were like bread sticks just out of the oven.

"Your choice."

"Do you know the famous story of Buridan's ass?" Montalbano asked him.

"No."

"Some guy by the name of Buridan owned an ass. One day he wanted to try an experiment. On the one hand he prepared a little stack of fresh hay, on the other, a pile of carob beans, and he put the ass between them. Unable to choose between the two things, both of which he liked a great deal, the animal stood there without moving, looking first to the right, and then to the left. And so, unable to make up his mind, he ended up starving to death."

Enzo removed the dish with the squid.

"What are you doing?"

"I'm leaving you the mullet. I wouldn't want you to die of starvation on me."

"What, you think I'm Buridan's ass or something? Put those squid back. I'll eat them after I've eaten the mullet."

A walk along the jetty therefore became a necessity.

Sitting on the flat rock under the lighthouse, he started reflecting on the whole affair, beginning with the unanswered question Augello had asked him.

What reason indeed did the killer have for running the enormous risk of keeping the corpse hidden, rather than get rid of such incontrovertible evidence immediately?

He sat there thinking about this for a spell, and in the end came to the only possible conclusion, which was that the discovery of Di Carlo's murdered body was supposed to constitute, for the killer, the last act of the show he was putting on. And therefore the whole thing had been organized according to a plan as contorted as it was intelligent, following a precise order. For this reason, finding Di Carlo's corpse was like the last tile of a mosaic — that is, one part of a whole.

But what was the whole? What did it consist of?

The inspector contemplated these two questions for a long time; then, since it was nearly time for their meeting, he went back to the station.

On the desk he found an envelope, addressed to him and marked *urgent personal & confidential*. There was no return address, but the postmark was stamped in Palermo and bore the previous day's date.

Fazio and Augello were sitting down and waiting for the meeting to begin. Politeness dictated that he should read the letter later, after the meeting, but that word, "urgent", on the envelope got the better of him.

"Excuse me just a minute," he said.

He opened the envelope and started reading. But then he immediately looked up and said to the two:

"This letter is about Di Carlo. It was sent yesterday from Palermo. I'll read it to you."

Dear Inspector Montalbano,

My name is Mario Costantino. I am the exclusive representative of the J Company in Sicily and live in Palermo at Via Ubaldo Carapezza, 15.

I am writing to you about Marcello Di Carlo. What I am about to tell may be of no importance whatsoever, but I still feel that it is my duty to bring it to your attention.

The day before yesterday, when passing through Vigàta, I went to see Di Carlo, long a client of mine, at his shop to ask if he had any new orders for me. I was unaware of all that had happened. And so I was told by the shop owners nearby that not only had his shop been set on fire, but that he had disappeared without a trace.

And so I immediately recalled something that happened to me last August 31. I was at Rome's Fiumicino airport, on my way back from my summer holiday. I was waiting to take the 5:30p.m. flight to Palermo, standing in the queue for the usual security check before entering the boarding area.

Just in front of me was a couple: a man of about forty and a blonde woman a few years younger. They were quarrelling in soft voices, but I still heard a few statements quite clearly.

He was asking her how a certain Giorgio had managed to learn that they were flying home that same day and was insistently accusing his companion of having informed this person. The woman kept denying it, practically in tears, asking him why she would ever have wanted to do such a thing. Every so often the man would say, as if to himself: "How am I ever going to get out of this? What am I going to tell him?"

At one point he turned towards his companion, allowing me to recognize him as Marcello Di Carlo. But since we were in a queue and he was distracted, he didn't see me, nor was I keen on him spotting me when he was in such an agitated state.

He did recognize me, however, in the boarding area and nodded to me in greeting. Then he and the woman stepped aside from everyone else and continued their wrangling. Once inside the aircraft, my seat was too far from theirs, and so I couldn't see them any more.

At Palermo airport, I saw Di Carlo again as we were heading towards the baggage claim area. He was now alone. We exchanged a few words about our respective holidays, but it was clear that Di Carlo's thoughts were elsewhere. At some point we were joined by the woman, who was very upset and out of breath, and who, paying no mind to my presence, said anxiously: "He's waiting for us outside. I saw him." Di Carlo stopped dead in his tracks. I said goodbye and kept on walking. Di Carlo didn't even return my goodbye.

That is what I had to tell you.

*I remain at your disposal for any and all
clarifications. I include here my telephone
numbers.*
  With regards,
  Mario Costantino

"And this means that Mr Bonfiglio has been feeding
us bullshit," was the inspector's comment. "But we'll
get back to that later. For now . . ."

"Before you start" — Mimì Augello cut him off — "I
have to tell you something that Anna brought to my
attention. On the twenty-eighth of July Bonfiglio wired
five thousand euros to Di Carlo."

"Only five thousand?"

"Only five thousand."

"But isn't five thousand a little insufficient for a
month-long holiday in Lanzarote, for someone used to
spending money hand over fist like Di Carlo, especially
since he's with another person?" asked Montalbano.

"Maybe he borrowed the rest from someone else,"
said Fazio.

The inspector went straight to the subject of greatest
interest to him.

"Listen up, guys. This morning we made a mistake.
We considered Di Carlo's murder, along with the fire in
his shop and his disappearance, as a separate case.
Whereas, in my opinion, it's all bound up with
everything else. In other words, until this morning, we
thought we were dealing with two parallel cases. On the
one hand the three abductions, and on the other, the
murder. And that's where we may have gone wrong."

160

"Explain why," said Augello.

"It is highly probable that the abductions and the murder are part of the same chain of events."

"What makes you say that?" Augello asked.

"The fact that the kidnapper, who has been the same person in all three abductions, used Di Carlo's car."

"But he may have stolen it."

"Then why didn't Di Carlo report the theft?" Montalbano retorted.

"But he'd gone on the lam!"

"No, Mimì. This business about him going on the lam of his own volition was dispensed with once and for all this morning. He didn't report the theft because he couldn't, having already been murdered and wrapped up by the kidnapper."

"Then why torch the car?"

"Because he no longer needs it. Di Carlo's car had made its last journey."

"And what would that have been?"

"Transporting Di Carlo's body to the place where it was found."

"Then what was the point of setting fire to the first car, the one he'd used for the first two kidnappings?"

"Mimì, I can answer that, even though I know I may be wrong. He set fire to it because it, too, had been used as a funeral hearse."

Instead of asking for which victim that car had been used as a hearse, Augello simply remained silent and thoughtful. Fazio buried his face in his hands.

Moments later Montalbano broke the silence.

"You're both thinking of the same person, right? The great absent woman, the ghost never seen. The girl from Lanzarote. The missing piece of the mosaic. We even thought that she hadn't come forward because she was complicit with Di Carlo; but now that we know that Di Carlo was murdered about a week ago, isn't it reasonable to think she may have met the same end?"

"Sorry," said Augello, "but I'm getting sick and tired of all these questions without answers, all these assumptions that then turn out to be wrong. You, Salvo, say you can't manage to see the whole picture, right? Well, then, just to have a starting point in common, tell us how you see things."

"OK. The three main characters in the overall picture are the so-called kidnapper —"

"Why do you refer to him as 'so-called'?" Augello interrupted. "He did carry out those three abductions!"

"That's true, but the abduction of the three women was not an end in itself; the only purpose of that was to throw us off. So, the three main characters are the so-called kidnapper, who is an intelligent, shrewd man who likes taking risks, Marcello Di Carlo, and the girl from Lanzarote.

"For reasons unknown to us, the kidnapper was overcome with intense hatred for Di Carlo. During Di Carlo's holiday, he devises a plan he considers perfect. He puts it into effect the same day that Di Carlo and the girl return from Lanzarote. He steals a car with a spacious boot and kidnaps his first victim, Enzo's niece. Then he kidnaps his second, that is, the Smerca girl. But these are dummy abductions, carried out simply to establish the bank lead as a red herring. All clear so far?"

"All clear," said Augello.

"Then he proceeds to kill Di Carlo and his girlfriend, possibly even at the girl's house. I would bet my family jewels that he didn't shoot the girl, however, but stabbed her to death. He then takes the keys to Di Carlo's shop from the corpse and sets fire to the place, leaving the apartment door open upstairs to muddy the waters and make us think it was the Mafia. Make sense to you so far?"

"Makes sense," said Augello.

"Then he takes Di Carlo's car, puts the two corpses in it, and hides it in a safe place. Then, once Di Carlo's body's been wrapped in plastic, he goes and dumps the girl's body somewhere, in such a way that she looks like the kidnapper's third victim. Except that something unexpected happens, which is that nobody discovers the dead girl. So he's forced to commit a substitute kidnapping, by abducting Luigia Jacono. Afterwards, seeing that the girl from Lanzarote's body still hasn't been discovered, he gets rid of Di Carlo's corpse, and that's the end of that. Have I been clear?"

"Quite clear," said Mimì. "There's just one small detail: of the three main characters, two have no names or faces."

"As far as I'm concerned," Montalbano retorted, "the so-called kidnapper is starting to look like someone we know."

"You mean Bonfiglio?" asked Fazio.

"Yes."

"Wait a second," Augello cut in. "What would be the motive, then, for the two murders and three kidnappings? And don't tell me that Bonfiglio may have lost his head because Di Carlo probably never paid him back the fifty-five thousand euros!"

"In fact I'm not telling you that."

"And so?"

"A man who does what this kidnapper has done must be possessed by a savage rage to be driven to such acts."

"But Bonfiglio and Di Carlo were hand in glove!"

"Mimì, hatred is the reverse side of love. It takes very little to flip the coin. Didn't the letter I just read to you tell you that Di Carlo was literally terrified at the idea of having to face his friend? At any rate, let's end here. We've already wasted enough breath. I'm going to Montelusa now, to talk to Pasquano. We'll meet again tomorrow morning at nine and try to devise a plan for dealing with Bonfiglio."

"Wouldn't it be better just to phone Pasquano?" asked Augello. "He may not even be in his office . . ."

"Well, if he's not there, it's not the end of the world. But when I'm talking to him face to face, I'm better able to domesticate him."

He pulled up in front of the Caffè Castiglione and bought a tray of six cannoli. Pasquano had a worse sweet tooth than a spoiled six-year-old, and the mere sight of the packet would predispose him to cooperate.

There was no traffic, and so it took very little time to reach the institute.

"Is the doctor in?"

164

"He's in his office."

"Is he in a meeting?"

"No, he's alone."

He knocked on the door. No answer. He knocked again.

Nothing. So he turned the knob and went in.

"Who told you you could come in?" Pasquano howled from behind his desk, where he was sitting holding a newspaper.

"I'm sorry, I thought I heard someone say come in. All right then, I'll just leave. Sorry to bother you," he said, holding the packet of pastries in full view.

Pasquano saw it at once.

"Well, since you're already here . . ." he muttered.

"Thanks," said Montalbano, quickly sitting down and putting the packet on his lap.

Pasquano got worried.

"If you do that you'll end up dropping that packet. And cannoli . . . they're cannoli, right?"

"Yes."

". . . Cannoli are very fragile. Put them on the desk."

"Well, I bought them for myself, but if you'd like to try one . . ." said Montalbano, holding the packet out to him.

Without answering, Pasquano snatched the packet, unwrapped it, took a cannolo, and started eating it.

When he'd finished, he closed his eyes, sighed, and said: "Exquisite."

Then, reaching towards the tray, he asked: "May I?"

"Go right ahead."

Pasquano wolfed down a second cannolo. Then he stood up, held out his hand to the inspector, and said:

"Thanks for the visit."

Montalbano was not discouraged. He shook the doctor's hand, picked up the tray with the four remaining cannoli, and started wrapping it. Halfway through the operation, Pasquano gave in.

"Did you come to ask me something?"

The inspector unwrapped the tray again and held it out for the doctor. Pasquano's hand shot out like the head of a snake and grabbed his third cannolo.

"Have you worked on this morning's corpse?"

"Yeth," the doctor replied with his mouth full.

"Care to give me advance notice of anything?"

Pasquano gestured with his hand for him to wait until he'd finished the cannolo. When he had, he said:

"Sorry, but my mouth is all dry."

He stood up, went over to a cupboard, opened it with a key he kept in his pocket, pulled out a bottle of Marsala, and, showing it to the inspector, said:

"Would you like a little?"

"No, thanks."

Pasquano set the bottle and a glass down on the desk, a clear sign that he had designs on the three surviving cannoli.

"What do you want to know?"

"How long ago did he die?"

"Let's say between six and eight days ago."

"How was he killed?"

166

"I confirm what I said to you this morning. A gunshot wound at the base of the skull, with the bullet exiting through his throat."

"So, if I'm not mistaken, this means that the bullet travelled downwards?"

"You continue to surprise me, Inspector. Despite your advanced age, your brain still functions sometimes. My compliments."

"Listen, is it possible the killer made him kneel before shooting him?"

"Yes, it's possible."

"So we're presumably looking at a Mafia execution?"

"Bah!"

"You have doubts?"

"Yes, because it was a small-calibre weapon, not the kind the Mafia normally uses."

"But do you have any idea what need the killer might have had to strip him naked?"

"I don't think it was the killer. These are very hot days. In my opinion, the victim was surprised in the middle of the night, while sleeping in the nude."

"What makes you say that?"

"Between the toes on his left foot I found a tiny thread of the fabric they make bedsheets out of."

"Did he have any other injuries?"

"No. There was a Z-shaped scar, however . . ."

"Yes, I know. Fazio saw it, which is what enabled us to identify him. Care to know who he is?"

"I really don't care."

For Pasquano, one corpse was as good as another.

Silence fell. Moments later, Pasquano spoke: "He'd gone to bed without showering first."

Montalbano looked at him but said nothing.

"Which is what allowed me to find the cotton thread. And there were also some hairs stuck to his sweaty body."

"Female?"

"Yes. Long and blonde, though there were a few of a strange colour as well. At least he didn't spend his last night alone."

CHAPTER
THIRTEEN

He got home sooner than expected that evening. It was still too early to eat. So early, in fact, that he didn't bother to look in either the oven or the fridge to see what Adelina had made, for fear of falling into temptation.

He sat on the veranda and lit a cigarette. The September evening was soothing and maternal. The moon was so round that it looked like a child's balloon suspended in air.

The horizon was dotted with the quivering lights of the fishermen's lamps.

A twinge of melancholy came over him at the thought that, in the past, he would surely have taken a long swim on an evening like this. Now it was out of the question.

And Livia, too . . . The last time he'd seen her, it had felt like a dagger in his heart. Wrinkles under her eyes, strands of white hair . . . How true were the lines of that poet he loved:

How heavy the snow weighs on these boughs.
How heavy the years on beloved brows.

[. . .]

The years of our youth are a thing of the past.

He roused himself. He was letting himself sink into self-pity, which is the one true sign of old age. Or was it not perhaps loneliness that was beginning to weigh on him, even more than the snow on the boughs?

He was better off devoting himself to the case at hand.

What could have caused Bonfiglio's friendship with Di Carlo to turn into hatred? The money transfers told us the friendship between the two had remained stable until the end of July, since Bonfiglio kept on lending him money. But the letter sent by Costantino tells us that on the thirty-first of August, at Rome's Fiumicino airport, Di Carlo was terrified by the prospect that his friend had learned the date of his return to Vigàta. What happened between July and August to cause the demise, or near demise, of their friendship?

Wait a second. The new element in the two men's relationship could only be the girl from Lanzarote with whom Di Carlo fell in love. Also according to Costantino, the girl already had a relationship with Bonfiglio, and in fact Di Carlo accused her of being the one who informed him when they would be returning. And that's not all. The girl knew him so well that at Palermo airport she went and looked to see whether Bonfiglio was waiting for them.

So perhaps Bonfiglio was telling the truth when he said that Di Carlo didn't want to tell him the girl's

170

name. And it was this very behaviour that aroused his suspicions.

And so Bonfiglio begins his own private investigation to find out who the girl is. Apparently he succeeds, and on the thirty-first of August he phones or sends a message to Di Carlo telling him that he will be waiting for the couple at Palermo airport, throwing them both into a panic.

And this means that the girl, by going with Di Carlo, had betrayed Bonfiglio, who must have been as much in love with her as Di Carlo was. And if that was really the way it was, it was more than enough reason to turn feelings of friendship into hatred.

At this point, Montalbano decided he'd earned a reward, so he got up and went into the kitchen. In the fridge he found a platter of cured-meat antipasti, and in the oven a double serving of aubergine *parmiggiani*.

He couldn't think of a better end to the day.

The following morning he got to work at a quarter past nine, due to the traffic. He immediately informed Augello and Fazio of what Pasquano had told him, and the conclusion he had drawn the previous evening.

"I also spent a long time thinking about things last night," said Augello. "In the current state of affairs, your suspicions about Bonfiglio are all rather well founded, but we haven't got a shred of evidence in hand. Any decent lawyer could make the prosecution's case collapse like a house of cards."

"So what do you suggest?"

"I'm not suggesting anything. I'm just telling you to be careful when you interrogate Bonfiglio. Basically treat him like someone well informed of the facts, not like the probable killer."

"Mimì, I can't just gloss over his lies."

"OK, but —"

The office door flew open and crashed against the wall with such a boom that all three of them leapt up in their chairs.

"Beggin' yer —" Catarella began.

But he couldn't finish his sentence because he was suddenly pushed aside by a young woman barging into the room. It was Michela Racco, Enzo the restaurateur's niece.

Clearly upset and fiery red in the face, she said: "I saw the man who kidnapped me!"

Fazio and Augello leapt to their feet.

"Where?" asked Montalbano.

"He was in a car that was coming into your car park!"

Mimì and Fazio ran out of the room.

"I was stopped at a traffic light when another car pulled up beside me. The man at the wheel was him, I'm positive it was, and I very nearly started screaming."

Mimì Augello returned.

"I'm sorry," he said to the girl, "but you weren't able to see his face, were you?"

"No, but the cap, the scarf, the dark glasses . . ."

"Where is he?" asked Montalbano.

"In the waiting room," said Mimì. "He's the person we've been waiting for."

"Thank you," Montalbano said to the girl. "But please don't tell anyone, not even your family, about this meeting."

"But why is Bonfiglio all done up like that?" Montalbano asked Augello.

"Because he's got a temperature of thirty-eight degrees," replied Augello.

"OK, tell Fazio to bring him in."

"Straightaway," said Mimì. "But please think it over, I beg you. If he's the killer, does it seem logical to you for him to come to the police station in kidnapper's garb?"

"And what if he really is the kidnapper, and he put on his garb, as you call it, just to lead someone like you to make the argument you've just made?" Montalbano replied.

Bonfiglio was holding his cap in his hand and had taken his sunglasses off and untied the scarf, so that it was now hanging down on both sides of his chest. But it was clear, from the flushed tone of the skin on his face, that he had a temperature. Fazio sat down on the little sofa, while Bonfiglio and Mimì took their places in the chairs in front of the desk.

Montalbano decided to take advantage of Bonfiglio's momentary weakness and started off by dealing him a heavy blow.

"I should start by giving you some news that hasn't leaked out yet. Bad news. Your friend Marcello Di

Carlo has been found dead, killed by a gunshot to the base of the skull."

Bonfiglio gave a start, closed his eyes, and began swaying in his chair so severely that Augello instinctively reached out with his hand to keep him from falling on the floor.

"Oh my God," he said. "Oh my God."

He ran his hands over his teary eyes, then wiped them on his trousers. Finally he reopened his eyes, heaved a big sigh, and looked directly at the inspector.

A flawless performance. Maybe he's expecting applause, Montalbano thought in admiration.

"Aren't you going to ask us who did it?"

Bonfiglio gave a wave of the hand as if to ward off the question.

"There would be no point," he said. "It was clearly the Mafia. I'd told him to pay the protection money, but he . . ."

"For your information, I must tell you that a series of circumstances have led us to rule out the Mafia as a possible suspect."

"But where was he killed?"

That question is a point against you, thought Montalbano. *You should have asked: If it wasn't the Mafia, then who was it?*

"Most likely at the home of his girlfriend, while they were sleeping," he replied.

But then Bonfiglio asked a question that had the same effect as if he'd exploded a bomb:

"And what about Silvana?"

174

As Fazio and Augello were exchanging bewildered glances, Montalbano suddenly remembered that Luigia Jacono had also mentioned that name to him.

If he answered the question, then the person calling the shots would be Bonfiglio, who had very shrewdly played the right card at the right moment.

This had to be avoided.

"Now that you mention Silvana," he said, "when did you find out that Di Carlo had fallen in love with your girlfriend, who apparently was equally in love with him?"

Bonfiglio didn't seem the least bit surprised.

"Silvana left for Tenerife in early July, and we spoke on the phone every day during the months of July and August. But then —"

"Excuse me for interrupting, but why didn't you go on holiday with your girlfriend?"

"Because my sister is ill. I didn't want to leave Sicily."

"Please continue."

"When Marcello first told me he'd fallen in love with a girl whose name he didn't want to reveal, I didn't suspect anything. Also because Silvana hid it very well and didn't show any change whatsoever in her relationship with me. Actually, if anything, she became more . . . more loving, that's the word. It was after she phoned me once from Lanzarote that the whole thing suddenly dawned on me. The strange coincidence of them both deciding to holiday in the Canary Islands . . . And then I got my confirmation."

"How?"

Bonfiglio tried to smile, but managed only a grimace. "I read somewhere that when we fall in love, our brains go to the dogs. Silvana forgot to take into account that I knew what hotel she would be staying at in Tenerife. And so I called them and they told me that she'd left on the last day of July."

"Was it a nasty blow?"

"I confess that I took it very hard. A double betrayal is hard to take, and hard to forgive."

"And you neither forgot nor forgave, it would seem."

Bonfiglio looked at him with a bewildered expression. "What do you mean by that?"

"That you lied to us several times."

"I did?!"

"If you keep denying it, it'll be worse for you. I'm telling you for your own good. You told us you hadn't seen Di Carlo when he got back from Lanzarote. Do you confirm that?"

"But . . ."

"Do you confirm it or not?"

Bonfiglio didn't answer right away. He was thinking very hard. Then he sighed deeply and said:

"I saw him the day he got back. He was with Silvana. I waited for them at Palermo airport."

"We know all about that. You called Di Carlo and told him you'd found out about everything. What happened in Palermo?"

"I was furious, I admit it. They'd taken me for a ride. She'd kept on calling me on the phone and sending me loving little messages while she was living it up with my

176

best friend, who, moreover, had only been able to join her in the Canaries because I'd lent him the money. I'd been hoodwinked like an idiot. I can only imagine how they laughed behind my back!"

"Tell me something: did you also give Silvana the money for her holiday?"

"No, she'd saved up for it herself, or so she said, at least. But now that I know what actually happened, I'm almost certain she got the money by other means, though it's anybody's guess how."

"Go on."

"I was blind with rage. I insulted Marcello, who knew perfectly well that as far as Silvana was concerned, I . . ."

He trailed off, as though embarrassed.

"Were you in love with her?"

"I don't know . . . It's possible. The point is that I had confided in Marcello about it, I'd told him how Silvana was becoming more and more indispensable to me with each passing day . . ."

"Did you threaten him?"

"Absolutely not."

"Did you ask him to return the money he owed you?"

"It was the last thing on my mind."

"What was Silvana doing as you two were arguing?"

"Standing to the side, crying."

"Then what?"

"Then, feeling afraid I might not be able to control myself any longer, I got in my car and drove away."

"Why did you fail to mention this meeting to us?"

"Because you called me in after Marcello's shop had been set on fire and he'd gone missing. I was afraid that if you found out I had strong feelings of resentment towards Marcello, that I hated him, you might think that I . . ."

"I understand. And in fact, Mr Bonfiglio, it's my duty to inform you that you are in a rather difficult position."

"What do you mean?"

"I mean just what I said. It's up to you to decide: shall we continue, or would you like your lawyer to be present?"

Bonfiglio thought this over for a moment.

"If you're not recording this, then it means it's not an interrogation, and so I don't need my lawyer."

"Thank you. Can you tell me how long you stayed in Palermo at your sister's place?"

"Until the day after I met Marcello at the airport, when my brother-in-law finally returned to Italy. He'd been abroad on a job, which was why I needed to be there."

"And where did you go next?"

"I came back to Vigàta."

"But the last time, you told us —"

"I was lying the last time."

"So how do we know you're not lying now?"

"Because you told me I'm in a difficult position. It's better if I tell you the truth."

"What did you do once you got back here?"

"For two days I holed up at home without seeing anyone. I needed to calm down in order to think clearly, so I could work out a way to get even."

178

"And then what?"

"Then, on the night of the second day, I got in my car and drove to Silvana's place. Marcello's Porsche was parked just inside the gate. So I had an idea. I went to a self-service station, filled two cans with petrol, and went back home. The next night, some time after two in the morning, I went back to Silvana's. My plan was to break a window of the Porsche, pour the petrol into it, and set it on fire. But the car was no longer there . . ."

He stopped.

"And so?" asked the inspector.

"I want to be totally sincere, even though I know what I'm about to say now will . . . In short, torching his car seemed in the end like a pointless gesture. I wanted to see them together . . . I had the keys to Silvana's house. I took a petrol can, opened the front door, went into the entrance hall without making any noise — I didn't even need to turn on the light because I knew the place by heart — went down the hallway, came to the bedroom but didn't go in, stood there for a while, then realized there was nobody there."

"So you didn't go into the bedroom?"

"I repeat: I did not go in."

"So how did you know there was no one there if, as you say, it was completely dark?"

"Well, it was almost three o'clock in the morning, there were no cars on the road, and it was absolutely silent . . . Normally when people are asleep you can hear them breathing, can't you? And then . . . there was something which . . . I don't know how to put it . . .

something I noticed . . . I don't know . . . a strange, sickly sweet smell . . . very disturbing. So I left."

He stopped. He got up and took a step, then turned back and collapsed in the chair. He buried his face in his hands, then raised his head and looked the inspector in the eye.

"Hard for you to believe that, isn't it?" he said.

Montalbano replied with another question.

"When you approached the bedroom with the petrol can in your hand, was your intention to burn them alive?"

"No," Bonfiglio replied at once, with assurance.

"Explain."

"It's one thing to torch a car, no matter how expensive, and it's another to set two human beings on fire."

"So what was your intention?"

"To sprinkle the bed with petrol and then let them see me with a lighted match in my hand. I wanted them to beg me to spare them, I wanted them to grovel at my feet, to humiliate themselves . . ."

"And that would have been enough to satisfy you?"

"I think so."

"Let's move on to another subject. Do you own a gun?"

"Yes. A Beretta 7.65mm."

"Have you got a permit for that?"

"Of course."

"Have you got it on you?"

"No. I carry it only when I'm going around with my jewellery samples."

"We were told that Di Carlo was very jealously possessive of his car and that you were the only person he lent it to. Is that true?"

"Yes."

"But don't you have a car of your own?"

"I do, but Marcello's car always made a better impression on the girls."

"Do you have only one current account, or do you have several?"

"I have three. My personal account is with the Credito Marittimo. The other two, where I deposit the earnings from the sale of jewels, are with the Banco Siculo and the Banca di Credito."

"Strange."

"Why?"

"The three girls who were kidnapped worked at those banks."

"You find that strange? If you run a check, you'll find that there are hundreds of customers at —"

"Do you know Luigia Jacono?"

"Of course. Not as a bank clerk, but as Marcello's ex-girlfriend."

"And do you know Manuela Smerca and Michela Racco personally?"

"Yes, they work at the Banca di Credito and the Banco Siculo. I sometimes joke around with them. So what?"

"Two of these girls won't rule out that you might be the one who kidnapped them. As you can see, I'm laying my cards down on the table, too."

Bonfiglio started laughing.

"And what reason would I have for kidnapping young women?"

Montalbano chose not to answer.

"I would appreciate a clarification. During the time you were holed up at home, did you never go out?"

"No, not once."

"So did you fast?"

"I didn't have much appetite, but, no, I didn't fast."

"Did you order food from outside?"

"No, I had tinned food, bread sticks, crackers, that kind of thing."

"Did you have any visitors?"

"I didn't want to see anyone."

"And your neighbours didn't . . ."

"I don't think they realized I was there."

"But you must have turned on the lights in the evening!"

"No, I preferred being in the dark."

"Did you get any phone calls?"

"Let me try and remember . . . Yes. Just one, from my accountant, the same morning I got back to Vigàta."

"We're in a bad way, sir. You have no alibi."

"I realize that."

"And do you also realize you've lost Silvana along the way?"

Bonfiglio looked at him in confusion. "I don't understand."

"When I told you that Di Carlo had probably been murdered at the girl's house, you asked: 'What about Silvana?' After which, you haven't brought her up again. Why not?"

"It was you, with all your questions, who —"

"What's Silvana's last name?"

"Romano."

"Age?"

"Thirty-six."

"Where did you meet her?"

"At my accountant's office."

"Where does she live?"

"In Via Fratelli Rosselli, 2."

"Shall we go there now?"

CHAPTER
FOURTEEN

The suggestion, perhaps because it was made so suddenly and unexpectedly, caught everyone off guard, and they sat there for a moment in stunned silence. Montalbano clearly saw a negative expression forming on Bonfiglio's face.

The first to react was Fazio, who said:

"We can all fit in one car. Shall we take mine or Gallo's?"

"Let's take yours."

Now apparently resigned to having to go out, Bonfiglio, before leaving the station, put his cap back on and wrapped his scarf around his neck. Fazio got into the driver's seat with Augello beside him, while Montalbano and Bonfiglio settled into the backseat.

Bonfiglio explained that Via Fratelli Rosselli was at the far end of Marinella. The first part of the street ran parallel to the beach, then turned left into the countryside, climbing up a small hill featuring Villa Ricciotto, among other things. This villa, which the owners lived in only in the summer, had a small caretaker's cottage beside its grand entrance gate. The cottage, which was a bungalow, had three rooms, a bathroom, and a kitchen.

Silvana had been renting it for five years, ever since the caretaker had moved into the villa itself.

"But doesn't Silvana own a car?" asked Montalbano.

"No."

"So how does she go to work?"

"The circle line passes here. She's also got a moped."

"Where does she keep it?"

"In the evenings she puts it inside the gate, for which she has the key. There's not much traffic on this road. And at night nobody ever drives by. It would be very easy to steal it."

"The night you went into her house, was the moped there?"

"Yes, it was there."

They pulled up and got out of the car. The cottage looked like a toy house, just a little bigger. The small door had an even smaller window beside it, with its shutter closed, the whole behind an iron grate painted green.

"Have you got the keys?"

"Yes," said Bonfiglio, "including the one to the gate."

"How's that?"

"Silvana forgot to ask for them back and I forgot to give them back."

From his pocket he extracted a large set of keys, singled out a very small key, turned it four times in the lock, then did the same with a Yale key, and finally the door opened.

"Just a second," said Fazio. And he distributed rubber gloves to everyone.

"You go first," Montalbano said to him.

"Should I turn on the light or open the shutters?"

"Turn on all the lights."

"You can come in," Fazio said less than five minutes later.

In the entrance hall was a coat rack, a mirror, a small settee, and a corner cupboard with a vase of fake flowers in it.

Opposite the door was a corridor leading into the house. Montalbano immediately noticed some dark stains on the floor.

"Be careful not to step on those. I think they're bloodstains."

"I don't feel well," said Bonfiglio, stopping.

"Deal with it," Augello said to him, pushing him on.

The first room on the right was a dining room, and the room on the left was a small sitting room with a sofa bed.

All in perfect order.

Then, also on the left, there was a perfectly clean kitchen and, past that, a bathroom.

The last room on the right was the bedroom, and here things changed radically.

"I'm not going in," Bonfiglio said in a high-pitched voice as soon as he caught a glimpse of the room.

And he remained standing in the hallway, staring at the wall, his face as red as a tomato.

The room had a wardrobe with a mirror on the door, parallel to the double bed. Then there was a small dressing table with another mirror and creams, perfumes, and other assorted jars on it.

On either side of the bed was a chair, near the foot, both upended and on the floor. One had men's clothes on it, the other some women's garments and underwear.

On the floor was also the lamp that should normally have been on the bedside table nearest the wardrobe.

The bed . . .

The couple had apparently been sleeping in the nude, without any sheet on top, so hot had it been those nights.

On one half of the bed was a large bloodstain, right under the pillow. Montalbano went and looked at it from up close.

And he saw the hole made by the bullet that had killed Di Carlo and was probably now inside the mattress. It was the position Di Carlo was sleeping in that had made the bullet travel in the fashion it had; he had not been made to kneel on the ground.

On the other half of the bed, where Silvana had been sleeping, he could see a great many tiny droplets of blood, as if it had been sprayed. But there was a great deal of blood, on the other hand, in the space between the bedside table and the wardrobe. It had not only left a big spot on the floor but had also spattered on the wall and the mirror.

But how had she been killed? Surely not by a gunshot, since there were no signs of this anywhere, nor by stabbing, otherwise there would have been much more blood everywhere.

Montalbano returned to the side where Di Carlo had slept.

"Have you got a torch?" he asked Fazio.

Fazio handed it to him. After making sure there were no stains on the floor in that spot, Montalbano knelt down to look under the bed.

The first thing he noticed was a cartridge case. Clearly from the shot fired at Di Carlo.

Then he saw a white rectangle that looked like an envelope. He crawled further into the space. It was indeed an envelope, and he could read the address on it:

Giorgio Bonfiglio, Esq.
Via Ragusa, 6
Vigàta (Montelusa)

He didn't touch it, but only crawled back out from under the bed.

Fazio and Augello looked at him questioningly, but he didn't want to say anything as long as Bonfiglio could hear.

"There's nothing more to see. Come with me." They all went out into the hallway. Bonfiglio was leaning against the wall with his eyes closed. It was clear that he had a high temperature and was having trouble standing up.

"Would you like to go home for the rest of the day?" Montalbano asked him.

"If I could . . ."

"Just answer me a few more questions and I'll let you go. As far as you know, did Silvana have a cleaning woman?"

"Silvana preferred to do her own housekeeping. Every Saturday morning, however, a woman would come and do a thorough clean."

"Do you know her name?"

"Grazia. I don't know her last name."

"Does she have the keys to the house?"

"I don't think so."

"Thank you for your help. Fazio, please take the gentleman back to the station to pick up his car, then come back here. On the way there, alert everyone to the situation here. Mimì, you go along with them, and stay at the station. I'll ring you there if I need you."

He led the way to the entrance and, once they'd gone out, closed the door behind them.

He needed to be alone to try to understand what that chamber of death had to say to him.

He found a chair in the sitting room, brought it into the bedroom, sat down, and contemplated the scene before him for many long minutes. It was as if he was looking at a stage set, though one still lacking actors.

And so he started trying to imagine how the double murder might have unfolded.

Marcello and Silvana have dinner at home . . . Sure about that?

No, he wasn't sure.

He got up and went into the kitchen. Above the sink, two dishes and two glasses had been set out to dry . . . But that didn't mean anything. They could have been washed ages ago . . . He opened the lower cupboards and found the bin. Raising the lid, he was assailed by a

189

stench of rot. It contained some leftover spaghetti and roast chicken, and some pear and apple peelings . . .

Yes, they had eaten at home.

He went and sat down again. Afterwards, they must have watched a little TV and then gone to bed. They'd taken their clothes off, made love, and fallen asleep.

At some late hour of the night, the killer enters the house without making the slightest noise. In his hand he's probably got a travel bag of some sort . . . Wait a second.

How did he get in?

The inspector had noticed from the start that the small front door bore no signs of forcing around the locks. And Bonfiglio had, moreover, opened the door with no trouble at all. Therefore the killer had used original keys, or well-made duplicates.

But how many sets of keys to that house were there in circulation?

He got up again and went into the entrance hall, where he'd seen Silvana's handbag on the settee. He grabbed it and opened it. Inside, among various other things, he found a small key and a Yale key together on a metal ring with a third key that must have been for the gate. He went and tried them in the door. They worked. He put them back in the handbag, returned to the bedroom, and sat down again.

But he immediately got up again, went to one of the fallen chairs, bent down to pick up Di Carlo's trousers, searched the pockets, and found the little key and the Yale and the third key to the gate, but no other sets of keys.

190

And yet Di Carlo should have had the keys to his house, shop, and car on him that night. If they weren't there, then the killer must have taken them.

But why had the killer left behind the keys to Silvana's house?

Easy: because he already had a set. He didn't need any extras.

Bonfiglio, for example, wouldn't have needed one.

Montalbano sat back down. Imagining the killer standing in the entranceway, he didn't want to give him Bonfiglio's face yet. It was still too early for that. It would be a mistake at this time, one that might lead him astray.

But one thing he was sure of: that despite the intense heat of those days, and those nights, the killer was wearing a jacket.

Because the jacket was necessary to hide the pistol he was carrying, and the torch he needed in order to see.

The torch was an absolute necessity. Even if the killer knew the apartment well, he didn't know what side Marcello would be sleeping on and what side Silvana.

Having put down his bag in the entranceway, the killer begins to advance slowly, on tiptoe, down the hall . . . He has all the time in the world . . . Still in darkness . . .

He reaches the spot where Montalbano's chair is, and stops there.

He now has the torch in hand. He turns it on, flashes the beam around the room, memorizes the position of the chairs and the two people sleeping, then turns it off.

He moves in slow motion along the foot of the bed, reaches out, touches the chair with Di Carlo's clothes on it, pushes it aside, then goes up to the head of the bed and touches the bedside table. He stops.

He hears the regular breathing of the sleeping couple.

Normally when people are asleep you can hear them breathing, can't you?

Isn't that what Bonfiglio said?

The killer now passes the torch into his left hand, and with his right he extracts the pistol, which is ready to fire. He'd made sure to load it before leaving home, to avoid anyone hearing the click of the metal when cocking it.

He turns on the torch and brings the barrel up to the head of the sleeping Marcello, who's lying on his stomach. He squeezes the trigger and turns off the torch.

The blast wakes up Silvana, who opens her eyes to total darkness and doesn't understand what is happening. Frightened, she asks:

"Marcello, what was that?"

The killer doesn't give her time to turn on the light on the bedside table, but leaps into the air, over Marcello's body, having meanwhile tossed the gun onto the bed, and, right arm extended, fist clenched, strikes the woman square in the face, smashing her nose. The blood sprays out. Silvana bolts out of bed, but with two

192

punches the killer sends her flying against the wall between the bedside table and the wardrobe.

A violent kick in the stomach sends her sliding across the floor, whereupon the killer grabs her by the hair, pulls her up onto her feet, holding her with one hand and punching her repeatedly with the other, taking pleasure each time his fist strikes her and sinks into her flesh.

And the savage pummelling goes on and on until the killer collapses, exhausted, onto the young woman's now lifeless body and lies there for a spell, panting, as just after having made love.

Stop right there.

Review what you have just imagined.

The killer shoots, turns off the torch, leaps over Marcello's lifeless body . . .

But why does he do that?

He could easily keep the torch on, point the gun at the girl, and shoot her dead . . . Or, rather, he could keep the gun trained on her, walk around the bed, and then start to . . . But why does he want to murder her with his own hands?

And why is he so keen not to waste even a second to take possession of her — indeed, to seize possession of Silvana's flesh with his hands?

Maybe because he's hungry for that flesh, or because he can no longer bear the thought of not destroying that flesh . . .

So if this reconstruction is correct, then the killer's aim was not to kill Marcello — who was just an obstacle to be eliminated, indeed to be leapt over, in order to get at his real target: Silvana.

Let us continue.

The killer gets up, turns on the light, still wearing his rubber gloves, and looks at himself in the wardrobe mirror. His jacket, shirt, trousers, and shoes have Silvana's blood spattered all over them.

He recovers the pistol and torch and puts them in a shopping bag he's brought along. He takes off his gloves and stuffs them into his pocket.

He then goes into the entrance hall, opens his travel bag, and takes out all its contents: a pair of trousers, a shirt, a pair of tennis shoes, and a pair of new gloves. He puts the shopping bag in the little suitcase along with his jacket, which he has removed in the meantime.

He puts on the new gloves, turns off the light in the entrance hall, and opens the front door. The car is as he left it, backed up against the front door, with its boot unlocked. He opens the boot, runs into the bedroom, picks up Silvana's corpse, and puts it into the boot, which he has lined with cellophane to prevent as much blood as possible from staining it. He does the same with Marcello's body.

He locks the boot, goes back into the house, locks the front door, returns to the bedroom and gets the keys to Marcello's shop, home, and car, goes into the bathroom, and looks at himself in the mirror. He takes the towel just inside the door, wraps it around his hand, turns on the tap in the sink, but does not wash his face; he only wipes away the spots of blood one by one with a corner of the moistened towel.

He then goes back into the entrance hall, takes off his shoes, shirt, and trousers, and stuffs them all into the travel bag. He puts on the clean set of clothing.

Then he starts roaming about the house, opening the drawers of the wardrobe, the small desk in the living room, and the two bedside tables . . . He takes all the photos with Silvana in them, whether alone or with others, as well as every letter, postcard, or document he can find . . . It all ends up in the suitcase.

Not only must Silvana's body disappear, but every trace of her existence, the very memory of her, must disappear. It has to be as if she'd never walked the face of this earth.

He closes the suitcase, opens the front door again, turns off all the lights, collects the suitcase, goes out, locks the front door with both keys, opens the car, puts the suitcase in the back seat, sits down at the wheel, and drives off.

It is still the middle of the night. He has plenty of time to come back and get Di Carlo's car.

Montalbano stood up, picked up the chair, and took it into the living room. He resumed thinking.

By the sight of it, Di Carlo's corpse must not have been wrapped in the room where he was killed, but in some safe place at the killer's complete disposal. Now, assuming that . . . The ringing of the doorbell gave him a start and pulled him out of his meditations. He went to open the door. It was Fazio.

"Did you summon the circus?"

"Yes, sir. But since there aren't any corpses here, I didn't call Pasquano. Prosecutor Tommaseo is on holiday; Dr Platania will be coming in his place."

They went into the living room and sat down. Fazio looked at the inspector and smiled.

"What is it?"

"Mind if I ask a question?"

"Go ahead."

"What was under the bed?"

"How did you know?"

"I could tell from your face."

"There was a cartridge case."

"Anything else?"

"Yes. There's also an envelope and probably a letter inside."

"Were you able to read the address?"

"Yes. It's addressed to Giorgio Bonfiglio."

"Shit! Did you read it when you were alone here?"

"No."

"Why not?"

"It's ninety-nine per cent certain that that letter is useless."

"What are you saying!"

"Think for a second. Bonfiglio had the keys to this place. He could come and go as he pleased."

"True."

Fazio paused and then went back on the attack.

"And what would be the one per cent chance that letter would be useful to us?"

"The date of the postmark. If the letter was written at the very end of August, it would mean that Bonfiglio probably received it on one of the first days of September. And it would constitute proof that he was here when Marcello and Silvana came back from Lanzarote."

"But he's already told us himself that he came here one night with a can full of petrol!"

"Yes, but he's always maintained that he didn't go into the bedroom that night, but remained in the doorway. Therefore, if the postmark on the letter is the right one — but only in that case — Bonfiglio has to tell us whether he came here twice or, if he only came that night with the petrol can, how the letter was able to fly in a curve to the right from the doorway where he was standing and end up under the bed."

Fazio changed the subject.

"You once said that you were almost certain that Silvana was stabbed to death. Whereas it would seem she was beaten to death with somebody's bare hands. What made you think of a knife?"

"It was a kind of free association of ideas. It's possible the knife wounds the killer inflicted on Luigia Jacono made me think of that, as well as the fact that Di Carlo was murdered by a gunshot. The difference in the treatment of the two victims indicates a difference of feeling towards them on the killer's part: revenge for Di Carlo, pure hatred for Silvana. The killer wanted to enjoy the pleasure of killing the woman with his bare hands, to feel her die."

The doorbell rang. Fazio went to open the door and returned moments later.

"They're all here: Forensics and Dr Platania. Should I go with them?"

"OK."

A few minutes later Platania came into the living room. He and Montalbano knew and liked each other.

"Feel like filling me in on this horror story? I'm completely in the dark."

It took Montalbano about an hour to tell him everything. Then Fazio returned.

"Forensics have finished."

"Did they find the letter that was under the bed?" asked Platania.

"Yes."

"Please bring it to me."

Fazio went out and returned with a plastic bag containing a letter. He handed it to the prosecutor, who opened it, took out the envelope, looked at the address, and read it.

"It's on the letterhead of Hermès Jewellers of Milan. They're informing Bonfiglio that the exhibition of the new collection for representatives only will be held on the twenty-ninth and thirtieth of September. The letter is dated August the twenty-ninth."

He put the sheet of paper back into the envelope, slipped the envelope back into the plastic bag, zipped it closed, and handed it to Fazio.

"Please return this to them."

That one per cent chance that Montalbano had mentioned might well turn out to have sealed Bonfiglio's fate.

CHAPTER
FIFTEEN

When Forensics had finished taking photos and samples and performing their various rituals and finally left, Platania suggested to Montalbano and Fazio that they stay a little longer at Silvana's house to discuss the best way to proceed with Bonfiglio.

"The fact that we still haven't found Silvana's body rather limits the investigation's sphere of action," he said. "The only relatively concrete piece of evidence we have against him is the letter we found under the bed. It is dated the twenty-ninth, but, unlikely as it would sound, he could claim he got it on the morning of the thirty-first, came here immediately afterwards, for whatever reason, and then left for Palermo in time for the couple's arrival from Lanzarote. This letter bears some weight, that is undeniable, but not so much weight as to tip the scales against him."

Platania had a point.

"What do you suggest?" asked Montalbano.

"For now, that we play strictly by the rules, to avoid any objections being raised further down the line. This afternoon I'll personally send him a notice of investigation advising him to choose a lawyer, who should get in touch with me at once."

"Then what?"

"Immediately afterwards, I'll ask to interrogate Bonfiglio, and in the meantime I'll send you a search warrant for Bonfiglio's apartment and another to seize his car."

"Why?"

"What do you mean, why? Given the tremendous mess he's made, I'm hoping we'll find an article of clothing with bloodstains on it. Meanwhile Forensics can check the boot to see —"

"I'm sorry, but I think a search will prove useless. Bonfiglio has had all the time in the world to get rid of everything he was wearing when he committed the murders and to remove all trace of blood in the boot."

"Well, I'm going to try just the same. Did you, Montalbano, say that Bonfiglio got inside using his own set of keys?"

"Yes."

"Did you make sure to confiscate those keys?"

He'd completely forgotten.

"I . . ."

"Already taken care of," said Fazio, pulling them out of his jacket pocket. "I had him turn them over to me when I gave him a lift."

For once, Montalbano wasn't miffed at hearing Fazio say, "Already taken care of."

"If we do as Platania says," said Fazio as he was driving the inspector to Enzo's, "we'll drown in a sea of red tape and waste a lot of time."

200

"Yeah, but in the meantime we can get a leg up on the red tape," Montalbano retorted.

"How's that?"

"He certainly didn't go about wrapping the corpse at Silvana's house, nor at his own place in town. We have to try and find out if Bonfiglio has some sort of isolated warehouse space or garage at his disposal, or maybe a summer home . . . It's very important we find out, and it's something you can do today, even this afternoon."

The trattoria's rolling shutter was halfway down. It really was too late.

"Anyone there?" the inspector asked, crouching under it.

"I'll be right with you, Inspector," Enzo called from inside, after recognizing Montalbano's voice.

He raised the shutter.

"Sorry to bother you, Enzo, but is there still time to get a bite to eat?"

"My wife and I are just now sitting down to eat, and we'd be honoured if you joined us."

After lunch, he went straight to the station. It was gone four o'clock.

"Is Inspector Augello in?"

"Yeah, 'e's onna premisses, Chief."

"Send him to me."

He filled Mimì in on the letter and Platania's decision.

When he'd finished, Mimì grimaced.

"Have you got a problem with something?"

"This story about the letter doesn't make sense to me."

"Why not?"

"Because of the way Bonfiglio is. You describe him as a lucid person, with a brain that works just fine, who weighs the pros and cons of every move he makes. And I, who've known him for a long time, agree with you."

"And so?"

"And so, even assuming he lost the letter, how is it that, careful as he is, he didn't notice that it was no longer in his possession? And if he did notice, then he would have to have realized he lost it at Silvana's house. So my question is: why didn't he just go back and get it? He had all the time he needed to."

"Your observations are correct if he lost the letter on the thirty-first of August, when Di Carlo and Silvana were on the plane to Rome. But if he lost the letter on the night he went to her house with the petrol can, or when he went to kill them, then there's no way he could have gone back to look for it without running a huge risk."

"That may be so, but such a huge mistake on Bonfiglio's part doesn't seem possible to me."

"And yet he made it."

Fazio came in.

"Chief, I remembered I had a friend at the provincial tax office, so I called him up. It turns out Bonfiglio doesn't own any other properties than the apartment he lives in."

"Why did you want to know?" asked Augello.

"I think he would have needed some place for wrapping up the corpse . . ."

Mimì started laughing.

"Oh, right! Just go for a drive in the country and you'll find dozens of abandoned farmhouses in ruins where you could perform a post-mortem on a corpse without any bother!"

This was true. The telephone rang.

"Ahh, Chief, 'ere's a jinnelman onna line 'ooz name I din't get but 'e says 'e was rescued, an' 'a'ss why 'e wants a talk t'yiz poissonally in poisson."

"Rescued from what?"

"I dunno, Chief."

The inspector didn't want to waste any time.

"Hello, Inspector Montalbano? Rescudo's the name, Michele Rescudo."

"Just a moment, please."

Covering the receiver with his hand, he asked Fazio: "Do you know anyone named Michele Rescudo?"

"Yes, I do. He works at the commune. I think he manages the tip at Piano Leone."

The inspector turned on the speakerphone. "What can I do for you, sir?"

"Inspector, I'm the person in charge of —"

"Yes, I know. Has something happened?"

"What's happened is, a few minutes ago, as the excavator was moving some stuff here at the tip, a big package broke and a corpse fell out of it."

"Male or female?"

"The body is in a pretty bad state, Inspector, and it's anybody's guess when it was brought here. Half of it's still inside the bag. But to judge from the hair, I'd say it's female."

Without being able to say why, Montalbano was immediately and utterly certain that they'd located Silvana's body.

"We'll be right there."

"Unless you absolutely need me," said Augello, "I'd rather not go. Every time I go anywhere near Piano Leone, I feel like throwing up."

"OK."

"Wait just one minute," said Fazio.

He went out and came back moments later wearing a pair of big fisherman's waders made of green rubber and holding a similar pair in his hand, which he held out for the inspector.

"Put these on," he said, "and be sure to tuck your trousers inside, like I've done."

The Piano Leone tip, which was located at the border of Vigàta's municipal territory with Montereale's, served five different towns, and before becoming a huge waste-disposal site had been a desolate *chiarchiaro* — that is, a barren, rocky expanse of scrubby sorghum bushes and prickly pears, completely unsuitable for farming and abandoned by all fauna except snakes and lizards.

Now, however, to make up for this, it was overpopulated with animals, including rats as big as cats, packs of wild, starving dogs, and many hundreds of seagulls who had sold their proud seafaring dignity to become miserable scroungers.

Before one could even see it, the tip announced its presence by its smell.

204

"Shut your window," said Fazio, who was driving.

Montalbano obeyed and then put on the small white face mask Fazio had handed to him.

When I get old and need assistance, thought Montalbano, *I'll take on Fazio as my live-in nurse.*

Rescudo, a fiftyish man with a moustache, was waiting for them at the main entrance.

"The body's not in this area. If you let me in the car, I'll take you there."

They drove along one edge of the tip for nearly a kilometre, and eventually Rescudo said:

"Stop here."

They got out. It was like being on the high bank of a lake made not of water but of smoky, muddy sludge.

Indeed here and there one could see dense black smoke rising from a grey sea of mostly gutted rubbish bags, out of which poured every kind of refuse imaginable, befouling the air and looking pestiferous to the touch.

"I know you're not going to like it, but we're going to have to go down there," said Rescudo. "Just follow me."

A short distance ahead there was a sort of path carved out between two mounds of rubbish. They went down the path in single file. Montalbano was terrified he might slip and end up with his head buried in filth.

At last they came to a clear area with an excavator stopped almost in the middle of a great mound of rubbish bags. A man in overalls came up to them.

"This is Vanni. He operates the excavator," said Rescudo, introducing him.

"How did you notice?" Montalbano asked Vanni.

"I'd scooped up a shovelful," said Vanni, "when a bag broke in midair and I saw first a big mass of blonde hair and then half a body fall out. So I lowered the shovel so that the bag with the body would remain on top."

"Let's go and have a look," said the inspector.

"Do you want to look from up close or from the driver's seat?" asked Vanni.

"From up close."

"Then wait just a few minutes."

Vanni went over to the excavator, turned it on, and began very slowly to reverse. Finally the machine emerged from the mound of rubbish. Montalbano and Fazio began to approach, with Rescudo following them. The inspector immediately noticed a streak of purple hair amid the mass of blonde, and no longer had any doubts.

Despite the advanced state of decomposition, the face still bore very visible signs of having been beaten severely.

It was hard to tell what she had looked like before. The face was so swollen that it seemed as if the killer had wanted to erase her very features. The same for her breasts and chest, which had been reduced to a formless mass of flesh.

Good thing the rest of the body was still inside the bag, because that would have been a hard sight to bear.

Fazio took several steps away, turned his back to the others, and vomited.

Then he came back beside the inspector. "Shall I inform everybody?"

206

"Yes, but tell Forensics to bring a generator, because pretty soon you won't be able to see anything here."

Fazio started making his phone calls. Rescudo dismissed Vanni and lit a cigar.

Montalbano likewise felt like smoking, but was afraid to remove his face mask. He looked over at Rescudo with a twinge of envy. Rescudo must have been an intelligent man, because he understood at once.

"Everyone gets used to it after a while, Inspector. Used to life and death, to stink and shit . . ."

The inspector could have sent for Gallo to pick him up, since there was no need for him to hang around until the circus arrived. Fazio would largely suffice. But it didn't seem right to leave; it would have been like one final insult to the poor woman, who, even if one admitted she had acted improperly, in no way deserved to die such a horrible death or to suffer such terrible disfigurement after her death.

But how, come to think of it, had she acted improperly? What had she done wrong, really?

Deceived Bonfiglio? So what?

She'd done nothing more than act according to the dictates of nature. Bonfiglio was almost thirty years older than her, whereas Di Carlo was almost the same age. With the little love messages she was sending Bonfiglio from Lanzarote, Silvana wasn't so much trying to deceive him as trying to buy time, to prevent him from becoming suspicious before they got back and Di Carlo had found the best way to lay everything out on the table and let him know that they had fallen in love and wanted to get married.

But things had gone wrong, and Bonfiglio, in a fit of rage, had gone to the airport to . . .

Wait. There was something here that didn't make sense.

In a fit of rage?

Are we so sure about that?

Bonfiglio spoke of a double betrayal. Of friendship and of love. But then, logically speaking, at the airport he should have had it out with both Marcello, a traitor in friendship, and Silvana, a traitor in love. Instead, he attacked Marcello and didn't say even a word to Silvana, who, according to his account, stood aside and cried.

No, that was no natural way to act. The scene recounted by Bonfiglio didn't make any sense.

So what was the explanation?

There was one plausible explanation. Bonfiglio had consciously forced himself to act that way and kept up the charade in his angry tirade against Di Carlo: never once addressing Silvana, ignoring her completely, as if she wasn't there, because if he'd had even the slightest contact with her, even just verbal contact, he might be unable to restrain himself and his hatred would have burst forth in a rage as unstoppable as a volcano.

He might even have gone so far as to kill her right then and there, before everyone's eyes, at the airport.

Something scurried fast between Montalbano's feet, interrupting his train of thought. He leapt in the air. Rescudo smiled.

"That was a rat," he said. "Now the sun's gone down, they're starting to come out. If we stay here, they'll eat us alive. You two'd better get back in your car."

And just leave that poor body there to be torn apart? How much more would it be made to suffer, even after death?

"But the rats might . . ."

"Oh, don't worry about the body, sir, I'll still be here. I'm going to start the excavator again, so the noise keeps them away."

Climbing back up to the edge was like resurfacing from a Dantean circle of Hell.

They slipped back into the car with the windows shut tight. Little by little the last light of day faded. The inspector remembered an old comedy by an Italian writer according to whom the next Great Flood would be created not by rain from the heavens but when all the toilets and sewers of the world started spewing out all the muck that had been thrown into them over the centuries, and that was how mankind would end, drowned in its own excrement. At the time it had seemed to him a work of the imagination, but now he was starting to have his doubts.

By the time he got back to the station it was after ten o'clock. Pasquano had deigned only to say that the time of death went back at least a week, and even he, in the face of that mangled body, had felt the need to restrain himself and hadn't uttered a single obscenity.

There hadn't been anything for Forensics to do except to take the rubbish bag away with them. It was just a formality, since they were sure to find more fingerprints than they would know what to do with.

Prosecutor Platania, on the other hand, informed Montalbano that Bonfiglio had been issued his notification, chosen a lawyer by the name of Laspina, and agreed to be interrogated the following morning at nine-thirty in his own home, since he still had a bit of a temperature.

"Do I need to be there?" asked Montalbano.

"Of course. Actually, it would be best if you yourself carried out the bulk of the interrogation, since you've already been talking to him. This time, however, we're going to write it all down."

"And what about the search warrants?"

"I've given up on that. Your arguments convinced me it would just be a waste of time."

"It might not be a bad idea to keep the news that we've found the body from going public," said Montalbano. "At least until after we've interrogated Bonfiglio."

"I agree."

He didn't make it home till after eleven. He wasn't in any condition to eat anything; if he put anything in his mouth he was sure to throw it up again.

What he felt, on the other hand, was a tremendous need to wash himself thoroughly. After having a shower, he sat on the veranda, with whisky and cigarettes within reach.

He wanted to devote some thought to interrogating Bonfiglio, which he would have to do the following day.

There wasn't any doubt that the man's malaise in Silvana's house was genuine. After venting his hatred as he'd done, emptying himself out entirely, he couldn't tolerate going back to the place where he'd killed two people. There, that was a possible starting point: take Bonfiglio back to his nervous tension of that morning, when he'd refused to go into the bedroom. And for this reason, use the same approach as in the prior interrogation, when he'd started things off by informing Bonfiglio that they'd found Di Carlo's corpse. This time, however, it was about Silvana, his last great love, and therefore his reaction would be completely different. Bonfiglio had pretended to cry over Marcello, but over Silvana he would cry in earnest, especially if Montalbano was able to describe to him the condition to which the girl's body had been reduced.

The phone rang. He went and answered, thinking it was Livia. Instead, he was greeted by the voice of Guttadauro the lawyer and Mafia adviser, who was always very ceremonious in his dealings with the inspector.

"My dear Inspector, it's been so long since I last had the pleasure of hearing your voice that I couldn't resist calling you, despite the late hour. How are you, my dear sir?"

"I'm fine, thanks. And yourself?"

"I can't complain. I imagine you're rather busy these days with the case of that businessman Di Carlo's murder . . . They said on TV that the body had been found, correct?"

"Yes, that's correct. He was killed by a single gunshot at the base of the skull."

"So that would mean a Mafia-style execution?"

"That's what they want us to think."

"I see. But you, sharp as a knife as always, weren't fooled by appearances."

"No, I didn't fall for it."

"We didn't think you would. Never be fooled by appearances! A good rule to live by."

That royal "we" was supposed to mean that he wasn't speaking for himself alone. Montalbano decided the conversation had gone on for too long.

"Well, sir, now that you've had the pleasure of hearing my voice . . ."

"Forgive me, good sir, I won't keep you any longer. Have a good night."

"And a good night to you, too."

So, through the lawyer's mouth, the Mafia had wanted him to know that they had nothing to do with Di Carlo's death. Montalbano, of course, had known this from the start. But why had Guttadauro so emphasized appearances?

What was he trying to tell him?

CHAPTER
SIXTEEN

The following morning Platania came to the station at nine o'clock sharp with a man dressed all in black and wearing thick-lensed glasses, whose name was Garofalo. He was supposed to record the minutes of the interrogation.

The inspector asked the prosecutor if it was all right to have Fazio come along, too. He wouldn't be present for the interrogation but would remain available nearby.

"Why, do you fear some kind of violent reaction on Bonfiglio's part?"

"Not at all. But he might be useful to us."

Platania had no objection to bringing Fazio along.

Since they had no other plans to work out, they got in their cars and drove off.

At number 6, Via Ragusa — a rather central street in town — stood an old four-storey building that had been entirely renovated a few years earlier.

There was no doorman or lift.

"Bonfiglio lives on the second floor," said Fazio.

They began climbing the stairs. There were two apartments on each floor. Fazio rang the doorbell to Bonfiglio's, and the door was opened by a reed-thin, sandy-haired man of about fifty, elegantly dressed.

"Please come in," said the man.

In the entrance hall he introduced himself as Emilio Laspina, Bonfiglio's lawyer. Montalbano had heard good things about him.

"My client still has a high temperature, but he didn't want to postpone the meeting. I hope you will take his cooperation into proper consideration in this affair. Please follow me."

The apartment had very large rooms, tall, airy windows, high ceilings, and a broad corridor. It was a structure from bygone days, when space wasn't measured in centimetres and walls were solid and thick. The living room was tastefully furnished.

Bonfiglio's condition had clearly taken a turn for the worse, and one could say the same for his nervous system as well.

He greeted everyone with a nod, but didn't open his mouth. His chin was trembling.

"Where shall we sit?" asked Laspina.

"You and your client," replied Platania, "can sit on the sofa; Inspector Montalbano and I will sit on those two armchairs beside it; and Garofalo can sit on that chair there and use the little table beside it."

"Before starting," Montalbano intervened, "it might be a good idea for Mr Bonfiglio to hand over to us the gun he told us he owned during one of our prior meetings."

"We anticipated such a request," said the lawyer, "and my client handed it over to me. You can find it in that case on the table. As far as I can tell, it has never fired a shot."

214

"We'll leave it to the Forensics lab to establish whether or not that's the case. Fazio, you take custody of the gun and wait for us in the entrance hall," said Montalbano.

Fazio took the case and left the room.

When the four of them had settled into their places, the inspector noticed how perfectly silent the room was; the noise of the street failed to penetrate the thick walls, and the building itself seemed uninhabited.

After slowly dictating his preliminary statements to Garofalo, Platania, with a quick glance, passed the ball to Montalbano.

"Mr Bonfiglio —" the inspector began.

"Just a moment," the lawyer interrupted. "My client was given a notice of investigation following an interrogation that was off the record. And all of this, moreover, without the presence of a lawyer. The whole procedure was unlawful. We have therefore two possibilities before us: either we repeat, on the record, the previous interrogation, or we do not record the present interrogation, either."

From a legal perspective, the lawyer's argument made perfect sense. But it put everything into question again. Montalbano had an inspiration.

"In the first case, then, we'll have to reconduct our search of Miss Romano's house and then draft a report of that, too."

Those were magic words. The very idea of having to return to that house, where he got so upset, made Bonfiglio start squirming on the sofa. Face as red as a

215

beetroot, he said to Laspina: "I'm never going back to that house, not even after I'm dead."

The lawyer gave him a strange look, as if bewildered.

But Bonfiglio's mind was made up.

"I want to get this all over with as quickly as possible," he said decisively, "and I really don't give a damn whether you record the interrogation or not. If these gentlemen wish to question me, I'm ready."

The lawyer turned to Platania.

"May I withdraw to another room with my client? I need to confer with him in private."

Bonfiglio intervened before the prosecutor could answer. "There's no point. I'm not going to change my position."

The lawyer threw up his hands in resignation.

"If that's what my client wants . . ."

"Then let's get started," said Platania.

The previous evening Montalbano had devised a plan for to how to proceed, but Bonfiglio's attitude suggested a different approach.

"Mr Bonfiglio, I'm not contesting anything you've already said, but I would like a clarification from you. I want you to tell us everything that happened between you, Di Carlo, and Miss Romano at Palermo airport on the afternoon of August the thirty-first."

"But I've already told you!"

"You gave us a general account. What I want you to do now is to tell us the same thing again, in as much detail as possible — with all the details you can remember, and the exact words that were said . . ."

216

Bonfiglio closed his eyes as if to concentrate better, then started talking with his eyes still shut.

"I knew they were going to have to take a taxi back to Vigàta from Palermo . . ."

"Were you armed?"

Bonfiglio suddenly reopened his eyes.

"I was totally unarmed. I believe I've already told you that the only time I travel with a weapon is when I have the jewel samples with me."

"Go on."

"And so I waited for them in the parking area. Then I saw them come out and look around."

"So you moved towards them first?"

"No, I stayed put. They spotted me almost right away, and then, after fretfully saying something to each other, they came towards me. Silvana was literally clinging to him, and she was white as a sheet and walking in fits and starts. She was clearly afraid."

"Did you use to quarrel a lot, when you were together?"

"Every now and then, like everybody else."

"Did you ever strike her?"

Bonfiglio replied with indignation:

"I have never struck a woman."

"So then why was she so afraid this time?"

"Because this time she'd really gone too far and she knew that I was in a state worse than she'd ever seen before . . ."

"Could you be more specific?"

"I was utterly beside myself."

He was sweating and took out a handkerchief to wipe his face, seeming lost in thought.

"Go on."

"I'm sorry. I didn't move. They came up to me and stopped. At that point Silvana said: 'Giorgio, please, I beg you,' or something like that. And she started crying. And I replied: 'Get out of the way, you slut, I'll deal with you later.' Marcello then immediately —"

"Are those the exact words you said to her?"

"Well, I don't know! How do you expect me to remember exactly what . . . I may have said 'whore' instead of 'slut', but the substance was the same . . ."

"Please continue."

"Marcello quickly pushed her aside and told me to be civilized. But I was . . ."

"Stop right there. Did you get a chance, afterwards, to talk to, insult, or argue directly with Silvana?"

"No, I never even looked at her again. As I said the last time, at a certain point, to avoid coming to blows with Marcello, I got back in my car and drove away."

"During our previous meeting you said you'd returned to Vigàta the following day and shut yourself up at home without ever going out. Is that true?"

"Yes."

"And yet nobody, not even your neighbours, is able to confirm your claim."

"Well, there's no doorman here, and I can't even hear the footsteps of the people upstairs . . ."

"All right. You claim you received only one phone call during those three days. Would you like to clarify?"

218

"There's nothing to clarify. I left Palermo at nine-thirty and was here two hours later. I was still unpacking when the phone rang. It was my accountant, who said he'd dialled the wrong number and apologized."

"How can you remember such a negligible phone call after all this time?"

"I remember it because I unplugged the phone immediately afterwards and turned off my mobile phone so that nobody else could call. I doubt my accountant would remember, but you can check with him, if you like. At any rate I don't see how something like that could be of any importance."

"That's up to us to decide," Platania intervened. "What's this accountant's name?"

"Virduzzo. Alfredo Virduzzo."

Montalbano gave a start.

Virduzzo! Well, well! Look where he resurfaces! Why had he never got back in touch? What had happened to him? Didn't he say he was going to write a letter?

Then all at once Montalbano remembered hearing someone say that Bonfiglio had first met Silvana at the office of his accountant.

Without wondering why, he decided it was important to confirm this.

"Did you first meet Silvana at Virduzzo's office?"

"Yes. When my former accountant, Deluca, died earlier this year, Virduzzo was recommended to me, and when I went to his office, I met —"

"What was Silvana's job there?"

Bonfiglio waited a few seconds before answering. "Officially, she was one of three women in his employ."

"What do you mean by 'officially'?"

"That she was a lot more than that."

"Was she Virduzzo's girlfriend?"

A hint of a smile appeared on Bonfiglio's lips. He shook his head.

"No, nothing like that."

"Then explain what you mean."

"Silvana was a distant relative of his and lost her parents when she was fifteen. She was an only child, and so Virduzzo, who'd always been a solitary, rather unsociable man, suddenly brought her into his house, paid for her to finish her studies, and began treating her and loving her like a daughter. He used to call her 'light of my life'. And their relationship, over time, always remained . . ."

He trailed off.

"Always remained?" asked Platania.

"I was about to say 'always remained unchanged', but that's not really true. Actually their relationship did change."

"Please clarify," said Montalbano.

"Well, after a while the idyll came to an end. It was when Silvana began to have her first boyfriends, her first love affairs . . . Virduzzo was worried that someone might take her away from him. He considered her his property. Poor Silvana had to resort to all kinds of bizarre subterfuges to enjoy a little freedom . . ."

"Then, if that's the way it was, why was Silvana no longer living with Virduzzo?"

"It was Virduzzo himself who rented a house for her after she graduated. But he had free access to her place. He even had a set of keys."

"And was Virduzzo aware of your relationship with her?"

Bonfiglio remained silent for a few moments before answering.

"Silvana was very careful. But I can't rule out that something might have come to his attention. And that would explain why I was sometimes forced to make sudden escapes in the middle of the night when Virduzzo would turn up unannounced."

"And why didn't you, Mr Bonfiglio, want Virduzzo to know about your relationship?"

"I'm sixty-two years old, Inspector, only two years younger than Virduzzo. Silvana was thirty-six. Don't you think that's a good enough reason? Virduzzo would have raised the roof . . ."

"Do you know we've found Silvana's body?"

Bonfiglio turned pale. A mild tremor began to shake his whole body.

He clenched his teeth and said nothing.

"The killer pummelled her with punches and kicks and then, after savagely ending her life, got rid of the body by tossing it into a rubbish tip. We literally had to tear it away from the rats to recover it."

The inspector had purposely laid it on thick.

Bonfiglio bent his whole body forward, buried his head in his hands, and began to emit a soft, continuous wail.

Then he muttered something incomprehensible.

"What did you say?" Platania asked him.

"He said, 'I'm so sorry,'" said Laspina.

"What are you sorry about? Tell us," Platania insisted.

Bonfiglio sat back up, looked at him, and replied with effort:

"I'm sorry I made . . ."

He stopped. Then he shook his head several times, as if to recover some semblance of lucidity.

"I'm sorry I wished for all those terrible things to happen to her," he said.

Montalbano decided it was time to fire the cannon. "Could you tell me when the meeting of the Hermès firm is scheduled to be held in Milan?"

Bonfiglio gave him a confused look. "What did you say?"

The inspector repeated the question. "Normally it's held in late September."

"What about this year?"

"I really can't tell you, because I still haven't received the letter announcing the dates. Why do you ask?"

"You haven't received it?" Platania pressed him.

"No, not yet."

"Are you sure?"

"If I say I —"

"The fact is that Inspector Montalbano has found this letter," Platania continued.

"Where?"

"Well, strangely enough, right under the bed in which Di Carlo and Miss Romano were murdered."

222

To everyone's surprise, Bonfiglio shot to his feet. He turned so red in the face that it looked like he was about to have a stroke.

"Show it to me!" he shouted.

"I can't. The Forensics lab has it."

"You're lying! Why do you want to ruin me? I never saw that letter! My God! I just don't understand how . . . You . . ." He was at a loss for words. Suddenly his legs buckled; he began to teeter wildly back and forth and would have fallen on the floor, unconscious, had Montalbano not caught him in time.

"The interrogation ends here," Laspina said angrily.

They went down the stairs in silence.

Montalbano felt confused and uneasy.

He'd come to Bonfiglio's place with the hope that the interrogation would resolve things, and here he was coming away with a whole slew of new doubts. Because all too often he'd clearly heard the ring of truth in Bonfiglio's words.

"Just a minute," he said as they were passing in front of the row of mailboxes in the front hall of the building. On the fourth one in the row was the name Bonfiglio. Montalbano stuck his hand into the slot, pulled, and the little door came open. There was no lock. Anyone at all could have taken whatever letters were in there.

Once they got back to the station, Platania wanted to have a few words alone with the inspector before heading back to Montelusa.

"On our way here," he said, "I got a phone call from Forensics. They found a great many overlapping fingerprints on both the envelope and the letter inside, so it's impossible to get a clear definition of any single one. It's a point against us."

"That's the least of our problems," said Montalbano. "What struck me most was Bonfiglio's attitude."

"What do you mean?"

"Well, he could have taken the pretext his lawyer offered him, but he didn't, and he didn't once refuse to answer any of our questions. Was he playing poker with us? I don't think so. Even the boldest gambler knows that luck eventually runs out."

"So how should we proceed?"

"Let's buy some time. If you agree, we can tell the lawyer that we're waiting for his client to recover completely before resuming the interrogation."

"That sounds like a good idea to me."

Since he hadn't felt like eating the previous evening, when he got to the trattoria he was as hungry as a wolf. To Enzo's great satisfaction, he gave it his all.

By the time he got up from the table, he felt as if he'd gained weight. Stepping outside, he noticed the wind had risen. He remained undecided for a moment. Then he realized that a walk along the jetty was an absolute necessity. He took it more slowly than usual, stopping every so often to look at the waves crashing against the breakwater.

He sat down on the flat rock and tried to light a cigarette, without success. The wind kept blowing out his lighter. He finally gave up and started thinking about things.

There was no point trying to hide it from himself. He'd set out with the firm conviction that Bonfiglio was the killer, and now, far from being certain, he was full of doubts. And this was because he had attributed imaginary actions to Bonfiglio in his mind. For example, he'd been sure that, at the airport, Bonfiglio hadn't spoken to Silvana, when in fact he had.

Another example: he was more than convinced that Bonfiglio would admit he'd lost the letter on the night he went to Silvana's house with the petrol can, and that it had been the killer who, in murdering his victims, had made it end up under the bed. This was a possible line of defence, and yet Bonfiglio had actually denied ever even receiving it. He wasn't telling a lie that was difficult to disprove; he was perhaps telling a truth that was almost impossible to verify.

To judge from appearances, however . . .

But what had Guttadauro the Mafia lawyer said? Never be fooled by appearances.

Want to bet the Mafia knew what had actually happened, knew who the killer was, and were trying to warn him that he was heading down the wrong path?

He got up from the rock feeling more unsure than ever. And anyway, truth be told, Bonfiglio had made a statement that had struck him like a blow. When he told him they'd found Silvana's body, and the condition it was in, the last thing he expected Bonfiglio to say was the words: "I'm sorry I wished for all those terrible things to happen to her."

They weren't the kinds of words that would come to the lips of someone who'd murdered a young woman with his bare hands.

He started the car but, instead of driving away, just sat there.

He felt disoriented and didn't know what to do.

Maybe — he admitted through clenched teeth — Pasquano was right when he said that he was getting too old and the time had come to retire. But he couldn't just leave the investigation hanging. He had to carry on. And since Pasquano was already on his mind, he decided to go and talk to him.

CHAPTER
SEVENTEEN

Half an hour later he was walking into the institute. "Is the doctor in?"

The usher and switchboard operator was probably daydreaming, because at the sound of Montalbano's voice he gave a start in his chair and took a few seconds to bring him into focus.

"Er . . . he's not back yet."

So the good doctor was taking things easy. Maybe, since he'd been wasting his nights at the club, he'd decided to have a postprandial siesta.

Montalbano decided to smoke a cigarette while waiting for him outside, but then in the doorway he nearly ran straight into Pasquano, who was just coming in. The doctor bowed and stepped aside.

"Please, please, don't let me prevent you from leaving. You have no idea how lovely the sight of your back is."

"I'm sorry to disappoint you, Doctor, but I wasn't leaving. I was just going to wait for you outside."

"I should warn you that I'm extremely busy and unfortunately can't see you right away."

"Please take your time, then. I can wait."

Pasquano threw in the towel.

"All right, come on."

And he trudged down the corridor to his office, cursing, with Montalbano following behind. They went in.

The doctor sat down behind his desk and started reading a memo. The inspector was about to sit down when Pasquano stopped him.

"No, please remain standing. That way we'll get it over with quickly and you'll get the hell out of here faster. What do you want?"

"You know perfectly well what I want."

"Then I'll be telegraphic about it. Death dates from quite a few days ago, how long I can't really say. I think she was killed at the same time as the man wrapped in cellophane. The girl was in a worse state than if she'd been run over by a truck. She didn't have a single internal organ still intact. The killer apparently lost all control and kept raging ferociously against the corpse long after death."

The inspector already knew these things, and therefore asked about what interested him most.

"Did you find anything that might be of help to me?"

"But wasn't it you who first identified her?"

"Yes, but every —"

"Didn't you see what kind of state the body was in? Total decomposition! A bit like you, my dear friend, with the sole difference that you, we don't know how, manage to pretend you're still alive."

Montalbano decided not to acknowledge the provocation, but rather to stroke the doctor's fur.

"But you, with your sharp eye and all your experience, I'm sure you must have discovered something that —"

Pasquano fell for it headfirst.

"Well, I can tell you one thing I won't put in writing because I'm not one hundred per cent sure of it. Actually, no, let's cut the Gordian knot and be done with it: I just won't tell you, and that way I won't have to worry about it."

The inspector was not discouraged. He well knew what Pasquano's weak point was. So he said distractedly:

"You know, as I was passing by the Caffè Castiglione this morning, I noticed they had something new . . ."

Hearing mention of the Castiglione, which greatly appealed to his tastes, Pasquano couldn't refrain from asking: "Something new?"

"They were preparing their sweets for the second of November a bit in advance. I *saw mostazzoli*, apple-branches, deadbones, marzipan fruits . . ."

Licking his lips like a little boy, the doctor looked him in the eye and said:

"I think — think, mind you, I'm not sure — I think I found some signs of synechia from a number of years ago."

Montalbano had no idea what he was talking about. "What's synechia?"

"In this case, it would be adhesions of tissue inside the uterus after some poorly executed scraping, preventing the woman from ever being able to conceive again."

"Let me get this straight: are you telling me the woman had an illegal, clandestine abortion?"

"So it would seem."

"But abortion has been legal in Italy for thirty-five years! Why didn't she just go to a clinic?"

"The answer to your question is simple. She didn't want anyone to know she was pregnant. And that brings our lovely little encounter to a close. I am hoping you are a man of your word."

"Have no fear. Tomorrow morning you'll be receiving a sampler tray."

While driving back to Vigàta, Montalbano came to the bitter conclusion that at this point there was a big hole in the investigation: Silvana.

What did they know about her? Almost nothing.

Of her thirty-six years of life, they barely knew a bit of what she'd done for her final six months. They knew, quite simply, that in this period she'd had two love affairs, with two men.

But what about before that?

How many men had she had, say, from the age of eighteen onwards? And, of these, which of them had she been in love with?

And which was the one who had got her pregnant? And why had she felt the need to have an abortion?

The explanation for doing it clandestinely was obvious: Virduzzo must never, in any circumstances, know about it.

So how were they going to find out more about Silvana? There was no point asking Virduzzo. Silvana would surely have kept her most important affairs, and the most significant events in her life, secret from him.

And so?

He had a good idea just as he was pulling up at the station.

As soon as he was inside he rang the Free Channel and asked for Zito.

"I've got some important news for you, Nicolò. We've found the body of Silvana Romano, Marcello Di Carlo's girlfriend."

"Was it also all wrapped up?"

"No, but it was put in a big rubbish bag and thrown into the Piano Leone tip."

"So I'm supposed to give this news and nothing else?"

"No, you must also say that we need as much information as we can get on her, and therefore anyone who knew her well should contact me. Then you have to tell a big fat lie, which is that there's a witness who claims to have seen the killer's face as he was throwing the bag with the body into the tip. In fact, he got such a good look at it that we've been able to put together an artist's reconstruction, which we will make public at the proper time."

Montalbano wanted to watch the Free Channel's eight o'clock news edition at the station, together with Augello and Fazio.

Nicolò Zito diligently did everything the inspector had asked him to do.

231

"You have to admit," Augello commented, "that looking for people who knew Silvana is a little absurd."

"Why?"

"You act as if she's an unknown person. Whereas all you have to do is call Virduzzo into the station to know everything there is to know about her. And he, moreover, is the one who should officially identify the body."

"I haven't called Virduzzo in for two reasons. The first is that I think there are a lot of things about Silvana that he doesn't know. The second is that Virduzzo has been acting in a totally illogical way, to say the least. First he says he wants to talk to me, then he disappears. I don't want to give him any rope. But I'm certain that now that it's been broadcast that we found Silvana's body, he'll get back in touch with us."

Montalbano then told the two about Pasquano's discovery of Silvana's botched abortion, and as he was just finishing, Augello's phone rang. Mimì listened for a moment, then passed the receiver to the inspector.

"It's Catarella," he said. "There's a call for you."

"Ahh, Chief, 'ere's a jinnelman onna line 'at wants a talk t'yiz an' 'is name is Paccanìa . . ."

Must be Platania.

"I'm sorry, Montalbano, but what's this business about an artist's reconstruction? And why wasn't I . . ."

Montalbano explained that none of it was true and that it was a trap he'd set, hoping it might prove useful. Then he hung up.

"As I was saying . . ." he began.

232

The phone rang again. Augello listened and then said: "It's Catarella again — another call for you."

"Ahh, Chief, Chief! Ahh, Chief! 'E's mad as a ratty-snake!"

This was the classic Catarellian litany for whenever Hizzoner the C'mishner was at the other end of the line.

"Put 'im on."

"Montalbano! Have you lost your mind? What's this about this artist's reconstruction nobody knows about?"

The inspector repeated the explanation he'd given to Platania, hung up, and opened his mouth to resume speaking, when the telephone rang again.

"Oh, what a pain in the arse!" said Augello, reaching for the phone.

He listened, then passed the receiver to Montalbano. "Catarella again, for you again."

"Ahh, Chief, 'ere'd a happen a be a lady onna line an' she —"

"Put 'er on."

"Hello, Inspector Montalbano? My name is Rita Cutaja."

She had the tremulous voice of a woman of a certain age who was trying to refrain from crying.

"What can I do for you, signora?"

"I just now saw on TV that Silvana was . . ."

Montalbano turned the speakerphone on.

The woman could no longer hold back and was now crying openly and having trouble speaking.

"I was . . . her colleague . . . we were friends . . . I've been trying for days to get her on the phone . . . Nobody seems to know anything . . . If you need information, I'm available . . ."

"Signora, if you don't feel up to coming to the station, I can come to you, even right away. As long as it's no bother to you. If you would give me your address . . ."

"Yes, all right . . . Corso Regione Siciliana, 149."

The inspector ended the call.

"You two want to come with me?"

"I do," said Fazio.

"I'll stay here in case any more phone calls come in, especially Virduzzo," said Augello.

"It's unfortunate you weren't able to hear Bonfiglio's interrogation," Montalbano said to Fazio as they were getting into the car. "I would have liked to know your opinion."

Fazio smiled.

"Actually I heard everything, Chief. As soon as the interrogation began, I went from the entrance and to the end of the hall and, since the living-room door was open, I was able to hear the whole thing."

"So what do you think?"

"What can I say, Chief? I don't feel I could bet the house on him being the killer. He defended himself damn well, that much is clear, but . . ."

"But?"

"I had the distinct impression that at one point — and only at that point — he was hiding something."

"Explain."

234

"It was when he changed the subject."

How does the human brain work? Montalbano wondered some time later, when thinking back on that moment.

It was when he changed the subject.

It suddenly came back to him that, at the most delicate moment of the interrogation, Bonfiglio had started to say something but then stopped, and when he resumed speaking he said something else.

And he, the inspector, hadn't noticed because he was concentrating so hard on the follow-up question.

"What did you say?" Platania asks, after not grasping what Bonfiglio has just muttered.

But the question is answered by the lawyer Laspina: "He said, 'I'm so sorry.'"

Platania doesn't let up: "What are you sorry about? Tell us!"

Finally Bonfiglio begins to speak: "I'm sorry I made . . ."

But then he trails off, and when he resumes moments later, he changes what he had started to say.

"I'm sorry I wished for all those terrible things to happen to her," he says.

So Fazio was right!

There's a huge difference between saying "I made" and "I wished" . . . Was Bonfiglio about to say he was sorry for something he'd done that had led to the girl's murder? And, if so, what could he have done?

And why had he stopped just in the nick of time, instead of finishing his sentence? Was he afraid of being charged as an accomplice?

And how might he have been about to finish his sentence?

I'm sorry I made such a terrible mistake? What terrible mistake?

"We're here," said Fazio.

"Huh?" muttered Montalbano, still lost in thought.

"We're at the house of that lady who called us."

I'm sorry I made that phone call?

And if it wasn't a phone call, what exactly had Bonfiglio made?

And what might he have said in that phone call that was awful enough to make him sorry afterwards?

"Chief, maybe you should get out, so I can manoeuvre better into the parking space."

Rita Cutaja was a woman of sixty-five who could have served as the typical female specimen of clerk who has spent a whole lifetime between files and dusty papers in offices with insufficient lighting and even less space.

Tidy in dress, tidy in personal appearance, tidy in her movements, she lived in a small, tidy apartment.

As she spoke, her eyes often filled with tears, which she wiped away with a small lace handkerchief. Before Montalbano could get to the matter at hand, she asked a question of her own.

"Have you spoken to Mr Virduzzo already?"

"No, not yet."

"Perhaps it would be best if you first —"

"Please let us decide that, signora."

"All right."

"When did you first meet Silvana?"

"When Mr Virduzzo brought her into the office and introduced her as a new employee."

"How old was she?"

"She was twenty-three and just graduated."

"When he brought her to the office, she had already been living with him for eight years. Did he never make any mention of her over all those years?"

"Never."

"So he never told you she was a distant relative who'd been orphaned at a young age and more or less adopted by him?"

"No."

"So how did you find this out?"

"Silvana told us herself."

"But how is that possible?"

"Apparently you don't know Virduzzo . . . He's never rude, mind you, but he's very closed and solitary, a man of few words. In all the years I've worked with him I only once saw him get really angry. In general he seems to have no feelings at all. A barren heart, you could say. He never married. Ever since his parents died, he's had a housekeeper to look after him, a woman who's now over eighty."

"But he did grow fond of Silvana."

"There's no denying that. But always in his strange way. She, poor thing, felt stifled by him."

"Can you explain a little better?"

"After she'd been at the office for a while, Silvana started confiding in me. I guess she saw me as a kind of surrogate mother . . . She used to tell me things she would never have told anyone else . . . That's why I'm in a position to answer your questions. Virduzzo saw her as a daughter, yes, but he himself acted more like her boss or her owner than like a father or a stepfather. Silvana was something that belonged to him, and he was very jealously protective of her. For example, when she had to go to Palermo to take an exam at the university, he would drive her there himself, or get the housekeeper to take her. He was so terribly possessive of her that eventually Silvana rebelled."

"How?"

"Well . . . at first she gained some autonomy by talking Virduzzo into buying her a house, where —"

"It wasn't rented?"

"No. I'm not sure why Silvana told everybody that, but it wasn't true . . . Then, almost for sport, or as a challenge, she started doing things right under his nose . . . It was very risky because he had the key to the place . . . But she always managed to get away with it, and would laugh about it with me."

"Did she have many boyfriends?"

"Well . . . yes."

"I have to ask you a delicate question. The post-mortem revealed that Silvana had undergone an abortion that —"

"That unfortunately left her sterile. I know everything."

"When did that happen?"

"Seven years ago. That time she didn't tell me anything until it was all over . . . It was the man who got her pregnant, whose name she didn't want to reveal, who organized the clandestine abortion . . ."

238

"But it seems to me rather unlikely that Virduzzo wouldn't —"

"Luckily Virduzzo had to go to Rome at the time, so there was no way for him to suspect anything . . . But, at any rate, Silvana's relationship with him changed just the same, afterwards . . ."

"How so?"

"She started to hate him."

"That seems a little excessive to me. Do you mean she detested him?"

"No, I know what I'm talking about. She hated him. She became obsessed with the idea that everything that had happened to her, including her barrenness, was his fault, for always having forced her to lie and hide things from him . . . He couldn't help but notice the change in her, and became embittered . . ."

"And how did that manifest itself?"

"He began to ignore her, and humiliated her by assigning the clients she had previously handled to others . . ."

"And how did Silvana take this?"

"She never said this to me, but I'm certain she hooked up with one of the office's clients, an older man by the name of Bonfiglio, only because she hoped Virduzzo would get wind of her affair and suffer because of it."

"Did she ever talk to you about Marcello Di Carlo?"

"Of course. It was Bonfiglio who introduced her to him. They fell in love and were very good at keeping it a secret from everyone. But, poor Silvana . . . She was caught between a rock and a hard place . . . Know what

I mean? Virduzzo on the one hand and Bonfiglio on the other . . . And so she worked out a way to spend a good month in peace and quiet with her true love . . ."

"Was it Silvana who organized the holiday in Tenerife?"

"Yes, she got the money from Virduzzo, hinting to him that there was an older man she wanted to get away from . . . In short, Virduzzo was quite happy to pay for her holiday, since he had no idea that Di Carlo would be joining her."

"So Virduzzo knew about Silvana's relationship with Bonfiglio?"

"I'm pretty sure he did."

"Tell me why you think so."

"One morning, when I was in his office, Mr Virduzzo got a phone call from a client. I think this person may have told him he ran into Silvana somewhere in Bonfiglio's company, because Virduzzo got very upset and asked what restaurant he'd seen them in and on what day. He angrily repeated Bonfiglio's name several times out loud. He'd turned pale as a corpse and ordered me to leave the room. That's the only time I've ever seen him lose his temper. I, naturally —"

"Thank you, you've been very kind," said Montalbano, suddenly standing up.

Both Fazio and Rita Cutaja looked at him in bewilderment. But the inspector was already heading for the door.

Back at the station, Augello was still waiting for them, even though it was already 10p.m.

"Virduzzo called," he said.

"What did he say?"

"He wanted to talk to you. He says he's available and that you can call him at home at any hour of the day."

"How did he seem? Upset? Was he crying?"

"No, he was neither upset nor crying, but his voice was cracking a little."

"OK. See you here tomorrow morning at nine."

CHAPTER
EIGHTEEN

Montalbano was left alone at the office. He needed to think things over a little, without anyone around.

The question was the following: should he act on what his instinct was telling him, or should he play entirely by the rules and keep Platania and Laspina the lawyer informed of his moves?

And what if his hunch proved to be yet another in a long string of mistakes made since the start of the investigation?

Would Platania overlook it as if it was nothing, or would he demand that he be replaced?

Because there was no hiding the fact that he'd got the culprit wrong; he'd become fixated on Bonfiglio as the culprit and charged full speed ahead, dragging the prosecutor along with him. And now that he was going to have to backtrack and point the finger at someone else, he could only imagine how much evidence and reconfirmation of the evidence Platania would demand before making any moves. But the hunch was the only thing which, if confirmed, would lead straight to the killer.

And this raised the classic question: was the game — which wasn't a game at all — worth the candle?

The answer came without hesitation.

Yes, it was.

He got up. The officer at the switchboard wished him a good night, and the inspector went out, got in his car, and drove off.

Fifteen minutes later he was pulling up outside Bonfiglio's building.

He got out of the car. The main door was closed and locked. He looked at his watch: ten-forty.

Too late, perhaps, to call on anyone unannounced. But since he was already here . . .

He pressed the buzzer. There was no answer. It was unlikely Bonfiglio was out. More likely he still had a temperature and had gone to bed. Montalbano pressed the buzzer again, and held it down a long time.

Finally Bonfiglio's voice rang out in a tone somewhere between surprised and irritated.

"Who's that?"

"It's Montalbano."

He imagined the man's shock, confusion, bewilderment, even fear. Bonfiglio quite likely imagined the inspector had come to arrest him.

"What . . . what do you want?"

"Could I please come up?"

"Tell me what you want."

"I want to talk to you in person, man to man, and above all without witnesses."

Bonfiglio made one last attempt to resist.

"I was just going to bed. I'm still ill and —"

"Mr Bonfiglio, I beg you. I know it's inconvenient, but I'll only take five minutes of your time."

Montalbano heard the click of the door latch unlocking.

He pushed the door open and went in.

Stopping in front of the row of mailboxes, he opened Bonfiglio's, found an electricity bill inside, put it back, and went upstairs.

Bonfiglio was waiting for him outside the open door to his apartment. He shook his hand and showed him into the living room. Montalbano noticed that Bonfiglio's face was even sallower than before, and that he had big bags under his eyes.

In fact he now looked older than his age. Was it possible he had more white hair on his head than that same morning? He sat down opposite the inspector and looked at him questioningly, without opening his mouth.

"Thank you for letting me in. As I said, and am keen to repeat, I'm here in my role as a police inspector, but not —"

"Not in an official capacity. I got that."

"I also wanted to tell you that I made a mistake."

"About what?"

"About you."

"Meaning?"

"I thought you were guilty."

"And now you don't?"

"No."

"Did something happen to make you change your mind?"

"Nothing new."

"So what was it?"

"I remembered something you said."

"Everything I've said is true."

"You're right. Even when you said you were sorry to wish all those terrible things on Silvana, you were speaking the truth."

"But if you think I —"

"The problem is that there's true and true," Montalbano said, interrupting him. "The truth of your regret for wishing terrible things on her served its purpose, which was to hide the truth of your regret for the terrible things actually done."

"But you just finished saying you consider me innocent!"

"That's not quite right. I never said you were *innocent*, I said I didn't think you were *guilty*, of double murder."

"What's the difference?"

"There's a huge difference. As you know perfectly well."

"I don't know what you're talking about."

"Perhaps you don't realize how serious the legal consequences of your position may be."

"Legal consequences?!"

"Yes. And don't try to bluff me. This is hardly a poker game. There's no way out of this for you: you'll be charged with either incitement to murder or aiding and abetting. The second is less serious than the first. And I bet you haven't even talked about it with your lawyer."

"Talked about what?! What should I have told him?"

"Still at it? You're disappointing me. I'm sorry, but I thought you would be a little quicker to realize that I was trying to get you out of this. But since you have no intention of cooperating, I guess I'll just have to ask Prosecutor Platania for authorization to request your telephone records."

This time it was Montalbano who was bluffing. It was anybody's guess whether it would even be possible to get his phone records, but Bonfiglio swallowed it hook, line, and sinker.

"All right," he said.

"You called Virduzzo?"

"Yes."

"When?"

"The same day I found out Silvana was with Marcello in Lanzarote."

"What was the date?"

"The twentieth or twenty-first of August, I don't remember."

"Did you call from here?"

"Yes."

"Did you tell him it was you calling?"

"Of course."

"Why did you do it?"

Bonfiglio shook his head.

"Oh ... At this point in time I couldn't even say why."

"Go ahead and try."

"Maybe because I was furious for having been deceived. Maybe I just wanted to vent my anger and scream; maybe I wanted Virduzzo to know the truth and punish Silvana however he could, maybe by firing her or making life difficult for her ..."

"How did Virduzzo react?"

"He didn't. He said nothing. He just sat there and listened, so that at one point I thought we had been cut off and started yelling, 'Hello! Hello!' but he just said, 'I'm still here.'"

"Who hung up first?"

"He did. At a certain point he interrupted me and said icily, 'Thank you for this information,' and then hung up." Bonfiglio ran his hands over his face, took a deep breath, and looked the inspector in the eye.

"You must believe me," he said, "when I say that at no time did I ever think that my phone call could . . . I haven't been able to sleep for many nights . . ."

"I do believe you."

"There's something else I wanted to tell you. If I failed to mention that phone call during the interrogation, it was not because I was afraid of being charged with incitement to murder, as you assumed, but because I thought I wouldn't be believed, especially by you, who seemed so convinced of my guilt. Between me saying I'd called Virduzzo and Virduzzo denying he received any phone calls, you would have believed Virduzzo. And if I'd started yelling that Virduzzo had put the letter under the bed to set me up, you wouldn't have believed that, either. You'd already condemned me. You'd stopped being a policeman and made yourself judge. Isn't that right?"

"Yes, that's right," the inspector admitted wearily.

Since he'd already come this far, he thought when he arrived back home, he might as well go all the way.

247

Going all the way meant sitting out on the veranda, duly equipped with whisky and cigarettes, and brainstorming, on an empty stomach, about what moves to make next. He had no evidence against Virduzzo, and it was going to be next to impossible to find any.

The only solution was to trick him into making a false move. To flush him out into the open.

But how?

He thought about this very hard for half an hour, without coming up with an answer.

A dark mood descended on him. The only thing to do was to go to bed, in the hope that he would have a clear head the following morning and manage to come up with a solution.

But in fact it was as he was brushing his teeth and looking at himself in the mirror that the thing to do appeared before his eyes in the glass, as sharp and clear as if it had been written on a blackboard.

At eight o'clock the following morning, after getting dressed to the nines and drinking two big mugs of coffee, he dialled the phone number for Virduzzo's house.

An elderly woman answered.

"This is Inspector Montalbano, police. I would like to speak to Mr Virduzzo."

"I'll go and get him."

"Good morning, Inspector. You beat me to it. I was waiting till nine o'clock to call you at your office. To tell you the truth, I was expecting you to inform me that my Silvana had been found."

Montalbano felt bewildered. The last thing he expected was to hear Virduzzo speaking in a steady, confident voice, with no trace of sorrow, whether genuine or fake. He immediately decided to follow him down the same path.

"If you want to hear me speak, then I'll be waiting for you at ten-thirty."

"That's fine with me. You'll have to tell me how I should proceed."

"In regard to what?"

"In regard to formally accusing Giorgio Bonfiglio with double murder. Anyway, I'm told in town that he's already been issued a notice of investigation."

Well, well. So the bastard was trying to pull a fast one by turning the tables!

"Have you got any proof?"

"Proof, no. But he gave himself away."

"How?"

"You must know of course that my Silvana left this Bonfiglio because she fell in love with a man named Di Carlo."

"Yes, I know."

"Do you also know that Silvana and Di Carlo spent the month of August together in Lanzarote?"

"Yes, I know that, too."

"But what you don't know is that Bonfiglio called me up in a rage to tell me that Silvana and Di Carlo were spending their holiday together. He was foaming at the mouth, insanely jealous, and said that he would kill them both with his bare hands."

"I'm sorry, but why didn't you tell me about this earlier?"

"But, Inspector! Have you forgot how many of our appointments were postponed? That was exactly what I wanted to talk to you about, and maybe, if I'd been able to, my Silvana would still be alive!"

"All right, I'll be waiting for you," said the inspector, cutting the conversation short.

As soon as he got to the office, Montalbano summoned Augello and Fazio to bring them up to speed on the situation. "With this move," he concluded, "Virduzzo is trying to throw the murder charge onto Bonfiglio's shoulders. It's an intelligent plan, conceived immediately after getting Bonfiglio's phone call, worked out down to the finest details, and applied with extreme cold-bloodedness. Just think, he kidnaps two young women to throw us off the scent, even before he's killed Silvana and Di Carlo. But since news of the kidnappings does not reach the public, once he's killed the two lovers, he carries out a third kidnapping, and this time the word gets out and makes some noise. And just to give you some idea of this killer's cold lucidity, don't forget that he calls me up to cancel an appointment at the very moment he has an abducted, unconscious Luigia Jacono on his hands. All the while he's waiting for Bonfiglio to come back from Palermo, verifies his whereabouts with a phone call, goes into his building, and takes a letter addressed to him. Then he kills the two lovers, after which he sets fire to Di Carlo's shop and sets the stage to make it look like Di Carlo has gone missing. And he does all this even while remaining in contact with me, claiming he wants to talk to me. If he'd succeeded in doing so, he would have told me how worried he was that he hadn't seen Silvana for some time and that he was afraid Bonfiglio might have harmed her in some way. And now he comes out with this charge against Bonfiglio."

"Maybe it's time to inform Prosecutor Platania of all this," said Fazio.

"I have another idea," said Montalbano. "We have one hour before Virduzzo shows up here. Fazio, I need a uniform from one of those private night-time security agencies for one of our officers to put on. Now, let me explain how this is supposed to play out."

Montalbano did not remember Virduzzo having looked the way he did that day.

Not that his physical appearance had changed that much. The wrinkles on his face were deeper, perhaps, but there was something quite different in his attitude. If, on the first occasion, his manner of speaking and moving seemed to belong to someone unsure of himself and insecure, now everything about him seemed to express self-assurance and decisiveness. He was dressed entirely in black, as used to be the custom for times of deep mourning.

Fazio was present for the encounter. Virduzzo shook their hands and sat down opposite the inspector.

"My most heartfelt condolences," said Montalbano.

"Thank you. I would have expected you to phone me before talking on television."

"You're right, but there was no time. After our phone call last night, are you still of a mind to accuse Giorgio Bonfiglio of the murder of your . . . your . . . What should I call her?"

Virduzzo's mouth twisted into a painful grimace.

"My daughter. I had adopted her, for all intents and purposes."

". . . For the murder of your daughter Silvana and her boyfriend?"

"I haven't changed my mind. On the contrary."

"How did you hear the news that the body had been found?"

"My housekeeper told me, after she'd heard it on television. I was already in bed. I've been rather unwell these last few days."

"I understand."

"No, you can't understand. What really drives me crazy is that if I'd been able to convey to you, Inspector, my fears that Bonfiglio might react in a murderous fashion, we would certainly have averted this horror."

"Yes, it's quite unfortunate . . . Did your housekeeper tell you where we found her?"

"Yes. That rascal threw her into the tip like some —"

"Had Silvana informed you of her engagement with Di Carlo?"

"Of course. Even if that wasn't exactly how it went."

"Oh? And so how did it go?"

"Well, last April, I think it was, I happened by chance to learn about my daughter's relationship with

252

Bonfiglio. Who I knew was a womanizer and, more importantly, almost as old as me. I made it clear to Silvana that I strongly disapproved. We had a rather heated argument. Then, in late May or early June, she told me out of the blue that she had broken up with Bonfiglio and felt like she needed a long rest. I was so happy to hear of these new developments that I offered her a two-month holiday at my expense. And so she left for Tenerife on the first of July. On the second of August she called me to tell me she was in Lanzarote and had met by chance a young man from Vigàta, of all places, whom I was sure to like. She told me his name and added that he owned an electronics shop . . . For the first time in her life, she seemed truly happy to me."

"Were you able to meet Silvana after she got back?"

"No, because she phoned me the very evening she got back — I think it was August the thirty-first — to tell me she wouldn't be coming into the office because she wanted to spend a few more days away from Vigàta with her boyfriend."

"Did your housekeeper tell you that a nightwatchman whose job is to patrol the tip to prevent any illegal dumping of toxic wastes saw the killer's face as he was getting rid of Silvana's body?"

For a few seconds Virduzzo visibly held his breath and hesitated before answering.

"No . . . she didn't . . ."

"In fact, he got such a good, close look at him that we've been able to put together an artist's reconstruction."

Virduzzo was having trouble speaking.

"But . . . but how . . . how could the killer not have noticed?"

"The nightwatchman was crouching behind a bush . . .When nature calls, you know . . ."

"But wasn't it dark?"

"It was. But there was a full moon, and the killer, moreover, was lit up by —"

"So he recognized Bonfiglio?" Virduzzo nervously interrupted him.

"Well, that's just the problem. In his opinion, it wasn't Bonfiglio. Which leaves us high and dry. We're having him look at a few people who knew your daughter. Actually, since you're here . . . Fazio, would you? . . ."

Fazio stood up and went out of the room. Virduzzo was visibly uneasy. He'd started sweating and kept his head down, eyes fixed on his shoes. Montalbano caught a whiff of a sour, unpleasant smell of sweat. A few minutes later, Fazio returned in the company of Augello and Officer Lovecchio, who was wearing the uniform of a private security company. Virduzzo didn't budge.

"Mr Virduzzo," said Montalbano, "would you please stand up?"

Virduzzo rose, keeping his head bowed all the while. Lovecchio cast a quick glance at the inspector and immediately understood the message Montalbano had sent him with his eyes.

"Mr Virduzzo, please look at Mr Cammarata," said the inspector.

254

The stench of sweat had become unbearable. Ever so slowly, as if it cost him tremendous effort, Virduzzo raised his head. The officer looked at him.

"No, it wasn't him," he said.

"Are you sure?"

"Absolutely sure."

"Thank you, you can go now. Mimì, you stay."

Virduzzo collapsed in his chair like a marionette whose strings had been suddenly cut.

"You'll have to forgive me, Mr Virduzzo," said Montalbano. "But this was just a formality that couldn't be avoided, though I already knew how it would turn out."

Virduzzo seemed to recover almost immediately. He straightened his shoulders and spoke again in a steady, self-assured tone of voice.

"I understand perfectly. No hard feelings," he said with a smile.

Now! the inspector said to himself. *Now that he's relaxing, now that he feels he's out of danger, now that he's lowered his defences . . .*

"Just tell me one thing," he said.

"Of course," said Virduzzo.

"Your housekeeper probably told you that the television report described how Silvana was killed . . ."

"Yes, she did. With the killer's bare hands. With punches and kicks."

"You're wrong," said the inspector, almost gently.

"About what?"

"The newsman never said how Silvana was killed, because he didn't know."

In a fraction of a second, everything came crashing down.

Virduzzo sprang to his feet and backpedalled until his back was to the wall, drawing a pistol with his right hand.

"Everybody freeze!" he ordered.

Despite the threat, Montalbano stood up. "Give me the gun!" he shouted.

By way of reply, Virduzzo shot at him, but the pistol misfired. Virduzzo didn't have time to fire again because Mimì Augello, who was the one closest to him, dealt him a powerful kick in the balls, and then a second, even harder kick square in the face as the man was doubled over in pain.

Fazio handcuffed him and pulled him to his feet. With his face now a bloody mask, Virduzzo started yelling:

"Silvana was mine! Mine! Can you understand that? She belonged to me!"

"Throw him into the holding cell," the inspector ordered.

"And she deserved to be killed like the slut she was!"

Virduzzo continued as Fazio and Augello dragged him out of the room.

Montalbano closed the door so he wouldn't have to hear him any more.

Author's Note

This is one of the very few cases of Montalbano's that did not grow out of a news story. As it is therefore entirely a product of my invention, it is unlikely that anyone would recognize him or herself in any of the characters or situations. Should this somehow come to pass, however, the responsibility for such an unfortunate occurrence will have to be attributed to chance.

Notes

page 34 **in Via dei Fiori there wasn't a flower to be seen for love or money:** *Fiore* (pl. *fiori*), in Italian, means "flower".

page 66 **"The cock's turned into a monkey!":** *Gallo*, in Italian, means "cock".

page 169 ***How heavy the snow weighs on these boughs*: From "Neve" (Snow), by Attilio Bertolucci (1911–2000), father of the well-known film-maker.**

page 229 **"They were preparing their sweets for the second of November a bit in advance. I saw *mostazzoli*, apple-branches, deadbones, marzipan fruits . . . ":** The second of November is *il giorno dei morti*, the "day of the dead", known as All Souls' Day in the English-speaking world, and on this day Italian pastry shops specialize in confections commemorating the day, with such things as sugary "death's heads", "deadbones", and so on.

Notes by Stephen Sartarelli

Other titles published by Ulverscroft:

THE PYRAMID OF MUD

Andrea Camilleri

It's been raining for days in Vigàta, and the persistent downpours have led to violent floods overtaking Inspector Montalbano's beloved hometown. It is on one of these endless grey days that a man, a Mr Giugiu Nicotra, is found dead, his body discovered in a large water main with a bullet in his back. The investigation is slow and slippery to start with, but when the inspector realizes that every clue he uncovers and every person he interviews is leading to the same place — the world of public spending, and with it, the Mafia — the case begins to pick up pace. But there's one question that keeps playing on Montalbano's mind: in his strange and untimely death, was Giugiu Nicotra trying to tell him something?

A NEST OF VIPERS

Andrea Camilleri

On what should be a quiet Sunday morning, Inspector Montalbano is called to a murder scene on the Sicilian coast. A man has discovered his father dead in his Vigàtan beach house: his body slumped on the dining-room floor, his morning coffee spilt across the table, and a single gunshot wound at the base of his skull. First appearances point to the son having the most to gain from his father's untimely death, a notion his sister can't help but reinforce. But when Montalbano delves deeper into the case, and learns of the dishonourable life the victim led, it soon becomes clear that half of Vigàta has a motive for his murder, and this won't be as simple as the inspector had once hoped . . .